Daphne tasted bette[r] remembered.

That was saying somethin[g] himself, he always drifted moments in her arms. He [pulled her] closer because she'd scared him, and he was very afraid he might not be able to keep her safe.

"Tell me what you were doing out there," he demanded.

"You know I was meant to meet an informant the other night when I got shot."

He kept his level stare on her.

"It happened in the alley behind the coffee shop."

"You should have mentioned that."

"I know." She rubbed her forehead with her injured arm and he saw her wince.

She could have gotten herself killed by running off. She needed to start thinking of the consequences. "It's dangerous for you right now. I'm here to protect you. Not judge you. Let me keep you safe."

She nodded. "I should explain it all when we are back at my place."

He wasn't sure what else she had to tell him, but he wanted to get away from this place and the scare they'd both had.

He'd gotten lucky that no one had been waiting for her.

Dear Reader,

Happy holidays! I'm so excited to bring you the third book in my Price Security series. We are back in Los Angeles this time, and all of the team are involved in helping protect Daphne Amana. She's a human rights lawyer who is working hard to return disputed antiquities to their countries of origin.

I've been obsessed with these stories in the news as well as the lucrative black market art deals and wanted a chance to include both in this book. Kenji and Daphne met when they were too young and too excited about the options in front of them to settle for a relationship. Both of them had a lot to prove to themselves and have managed to do that with long and successful careers.

But life puts them in each other's path again and they are different people now and want that second chance.

I hope you enjoy this book!

Happy reading,

Katherine

CHRISTMAS BODYGUARD

KATHERINE GARBERA

Harlequin

ROMANTIC SUSPENSE

If you purchased this book without a cover you should be aware that this book is stolen property. It was reported as "unsold and destroyed" to the publisher, and neither the author nor the publisher has received any payment for this "stripped book."

**Harlequin®
ROMANTIC
SUSPENSE™**

Recycling programs
for this product may
not exist in your area.

ISBN-13: 978-1-335-50251-3

Christmas Bodyguard

Copyright © 2024 by Katherine Garbera

All rights reserved. No part of this book may be used or reproduced in any manner whatsoever without written permission.

Without limiting the author's and publisher's exclusive rights, any unauthorized use of this publication to train generative artificial intelligence (AI) technologies is expressly prohibited.

This is a work of fiction. Names, characters, places and incidents are either the product of the author's imagination or are used fictitiously. Any resemblance to actual persons, living or dead, businesses, companies, events or locales is entirely coincidental.

For questions and comments about the quality of this book, please contact us at CustomerService@Harlequin.com.

TM and ® are trademarks of Harlequin Enterprises ULC.

Harlequin Enterprises ULC
22 Adelaide St. West, 41st Floor
Toronto, Ontario M5H 4E3, Canada
www.Harlequin.com

Printed in Lithuania

MIX
Paper | Supporting
responsible forestry
FSC® C021394

Katherine Garbera is a *USA TODAY* bestselling author of more than one hundred novels, which have been translated into over two dozen languages and sold millions of copies worldwide. She is the mother of two incredibly creative and snarky grown children. Katherine enjoys drinking champagne, reading, walking and traveling with her husband. She lives in Kent, UK, where she is working on her next novel. Visit her on the web at www.katherinegarbera.com.

Books by Katherine Garbera

Harlequin Romantic Suspense

Price Security

Bodyguard Most Wanted
Safe in Her Bodyguard's Arms
Christmas Bodyguard

Visit the Author Profile page
at Harlequin.com for more titles.

For Rob. Sharing our life together makes
every day an adventure. Love you.

Chapter 1

Daphne Amana was a leading attorney in international rights and criminal law. The company directory at Mitchell and Partners law firm described her as a brilliant mind who handled cases of real international importance. She was pretty sure her boss wouldn't see this as her most brilliant move. But she was out of options, so meeting an informant in a dark alley…well… might not be the safest decision, but it was the only play she had in this case. She was trying to return contested artifacts back to the village of Amba Mariam, the modern home of the Gondar tribe from Ethiopia.

The collection was part of items taken during the 1867 expedition of British and Indian soldiers with the stated aim of freeing British hostages and punishing Emperor Tewodros II and his people. The military assault was a success. Hundreds of items were pillaged by the soldiers, and many were sold at an auction where most of the collection that was housed at the British Museum was acquired. The only rival for its significance was the collection at the Los Angeles Museum of Foreign Cultures, which was donated by the grandson of one of the British soldiers and contained gold and silver regalia, jewelry, weapons and liturgical vessels and crosses from the Ethiopian Orthodox Church.

Daphne became aware of the collection at the Los Angeles Museum of Foreign Cultures when a cultural minister for Ethiopia, Marjorie Wyman, hired her law firm to petition to have the items returned when her discussions with the museum director stalled. Working in international rights gave Daphne a background that made this case one she wanted—no, needed—and she'd asked to be assigned to it. But the director of the Los Angeles Museum of Foreign Cultures, Pierce Lauder, was being difficult, and his attorneys kept asking for postponements of the actual trial that were making the discovery of the items still in the museum's collection difficult.

Daphne had taken the museum to court, gaining a motion to compel them to allow her access to their museum and storerooms, but still they were coming up with excuses for why she couldn't get in to inventory the items. Sure, it was the holiday season. Thanksgiving had been last week, so a lot of people had taken extra time off, herself included, but she could see through the flimsy excuse that Mr. Lauder kept providing.

Especially when the list of items he'd sent over marked several as *missing*. Not stolen or lost, simply missing. She'd gone on a local news show to make the public aware of the contested collection, which had stirred up interest and spawned several public protests, but still, Lauder wasn't returning her calls.

History had always been a passion of hers—the fact that many of the exhibits she'd enjoyed at places like the British Museum were taken as spoils of war had never seemed fair to her. It was part of the reason she'd become an international rights attorney.

The collection was a small one that had come to the Los Angeles Museum of Foreign Cultures by way of Jonathon Hazelton-Measham, who'd been part of the 1867 expeditionary force of British and Indian soldiers led by Sir Robert Napier into Maqdala, an almost impenetrable mountain fortress in northern Ethiopia that was the seat of power for Emperor Tewodros II. Tewodros had established a library and a treasury and dedicated a new church as part of his plan to unite the tribes of Ethiopia and create one united country.

The British had been helping Tewodros, including educating and training his son, when they had a falling out, which resulted in a massive assault on the fortress in 1868. It caused the deaths of hundreds of Tewodros's army with only limited British casualties. After the invasion, there was widespread looting of the fortress and church by soldiers.

Many of the pillaged objects were subsequently reassembled and auctioned. But Jonathon Hazelton-Measham kept the objects he'd collected, which included many items from the new church that had been constructed. The items, or tabots, included a silver censer used to burn incense during mass, a ceremonial cross, two chalices, and processional umbrella tops. He also had several weapons and regalia that were rumored to have come from the fortress. The thirty-nine items that Jonathon looted and brought home with him to England were sold via his descendants to the museum in 1985.

Of the thirty-nine items, the museum claimed that roughly twenty-five were still in their possession. Fourteen items either dropped off their inventory or were currently marked missing.

Her client represented the department of culture for Amba Mariam, the modern day name for Maqdala. The items weren't just in the Los Angeles Museum of Foreign Cultures but also in the British Museum. The bulk of the items still accounted for remained in England at different museums and libraries as well as a museum in Canada, all of which were holding ongoing discussions about their return to Amba Mariam.

Which didn't help Daphne's case. There was no precedent stating that the items should be returned. If the items had been returned in London, that would go a long way to swaying the judge to rule in her client's favor.

However, the recent theft of items by a complicit staff member at the British Museum was helping her with this case. There were only so many places to sell rare antiquities without raising suspicion.

The missing items included one chalice, the silver censer—apparently the brass censer was still in the museum's possession—a piece of regalia not named, two other tabots, and a diptych in a silver case that may have come from a private collection in France, which suggested to Daphne that the thief knew the value of what they were taking. Then there were two manuscripts that were described in the late Hazelton-Measham's will as part of his donation but had been dropped from the museum's inventory in the 2010s before the current director was in place.

It wasn't the monetary value that was at the heart of this case as far as Daphne was concerned. It was the cultural value. Emperor Tewodros II had collected these items from all of the tribes of Ethiopia to unite them into one kingdom.

Apparently there had been flooding at the museum, and some of the pieces had been lost during the evacuation of items. Which wasn't a suitable response as far as Daphne was concerned. Museums were sticklers for cataloging their priceless antiquities. She'd been going round and round with Pierce Lauder and his lawyer, Ben Cross, ever since, trying to figure out what happened to the mysterious missing pieces.

Which was didn't explain why she was sitting in her car at nine p.m., trying to get up the courage to go and meet an anonymous person who had messaged her on WhatsApp, saying that they had information on the missing items.

She'd tried to convince them to come to her office, but they'd been insistent they would only meet her away from both the museum and her offices. She'd suggested a twenty-four-hour coffee shop that she frequented, Zara's Brew on North Hollywood Boulevard. Her informant had agreed to her request, but they wanted to meet behind the shop so they wouldn't be observed.

She was a single woman who could protect herself, but still, this had *bad idea* written all over it. She knew Carl would have forbidden her to do it and probably would have removed her from the case entirely, so she hadn't let anyone know she was here. Which now seemed…well, not like her best idea. So she texted her assistant just to say she was meeting an informant and gave her location. She also held her phone in her hand with 911 ready in case things got dicey.

She left her car and hit the lock button as she walked

toward the coffee shop. The barista on duty had their head down scrolling on their phone, and there were only two diners in the café area. She took a deep breath as she headed around the back of the shop and saw that the alleyway was empty and dimly lit.

Because of course it was. Right?

Pulling the strap of her purse higher on her shoulder, she moved into the alley.

"Hello?" she called.

Stepping further into the alleyway, Daphne cautiously scanned the area. A shot rang out, and she felt the impact of the bullet in her shoulder. There was a sharp burning pain and she bit her lip to keep from crying out. God. That hurt. She hit 911 as she fell to the ground, trying blend with the shadows near the dumpster. She felt woozy and scared, and started the deep breathing exercises she'd learned to keep from passing out because she had a low blood pressure condition that gave her dizzy spells.

"911, what's your emergency?"

She heard the sound of footsteps running away and a thud. Glancing toward the sound, she didn't see anyone.

"I've been shot. I'm behind Zara's Brew. I got hit in the shoulder and am bleeding. I can't see who shot me."

"Stay on the line. I'm dispatching police and ambulance to your location."

Daphne leaned against the dumpster, keeping her legs close to her body, her head tipped back as she held the line. The 911 operator kept talking to her, and Daphne always responded, but she knew she was close to losing the battle to stay conscious. She reached for her purse to get a tissue to apply pressure to her shoulder.

She fumbled when opening it, and some of the contents spilled out on the dirty pavement. After a moment, she found the tissues and pressed one against her shoulder, then put her phone on speaker, setting it on her lap. She glanced around, realizing that her wallet had fallen out.

Placing the bloody tissue on her lap, she reached for the wallet and other items, and she noticed something that looked like a burlap bag with the museum logo on it. She pulled it toward her just as the cops parked at the end of the alley. She shoved the bag into her purse along with her wallet.

"I'm over here," she said.

Two cops came toward her location. One of them was on alert, gun drawn.

"I'm unarmed and injured," she said.

"Don't worry, ma'am, the ambulance will be here in a moment. Where are you hurt?"

"Shoulder," she said. She was starting to slur her words as the pain became too much. Her last conscious thought before she passed out was to draw her purse to her body. "Don't…leave…my…bag…behind."

"I won't. We've got you."

The world faded to black. She was semiconscious of being loaded onto stretcher and transported to the hospital. She was still in pain and still scared, but she knew that whatever was in that burlap museum bag was worth it. After all this time, she might have finally gotten a break in the case that would help her figure out why the museum had stopped talking with her and the cultural minister. What really happened to the missing artifacts?

* * *

Working for Price Security gave Kenji Wada a chance to use the skills he'd honed for nearly a decade in the CIA as a field operative. The job had been exciting, and there had been a few life-and-death moments, which suited Kenji's need for adrenaline rushes. But he'd retired after a case had gone sour. And when Giovanni "Van" Price had offered him a job working as a bodyguard at his elite company, Kenji had said yes.

He was Japanese American, raised by his single American mother. He didn't know much about his Japanese heritage except that his father's family was from a highly traditional background of wealth and status and hadn't approved of her. They hadn't been allowed to marry, so his mom had said deuces to his old man and came back to LA, where she'd raised him. He had been close to his mom from the beginning and had nothing but love and respect for her. But he always had questions about half of his lineage and no one to ask since his mom had died several years ago when he'd been overseas on an assignment. He still missed her.

Something he didn't like to dwell on.

As he waited for the latest briefing at Price to start, he knew that he was going to volunteer for whatever new assignment came up. Didn't matter that it was the start of December. Christmas wasn't his favorite time of year. It had always been a struggle for his mom to buy him presents, pay the bills and keep food on the table. She'd always made the holiday special and since he'd lost her… Christmas just felt empty. If Kenji had his way, he'd work through the holidays. He needed to stay busy and focused on the job. Not his personal life.

The others on the team arrived for the meeting. The Price Security team was small and tight. Van liked to say they were a family, and Kenji did view the other members like siblings. They all got along for the most part but also got on each other's nerves at times.

There were two women on the team. Luna Urban-DeVere was a former MMA fighter, wickedly smart and tough as nails. She was married to multimillionaire Nicholas DeVere, who she met while protecting him. Lee Oscar was the tech genius of their team, and though she had skills with weapons and hand-to-hand combat, most of the time she stayed here in the Price Tower, keeping tabs on the team and providing information to them.

Next was Rick Stone, a former DEA agent who always looked like he was about to fall asleep until there was danger—and then he turned lethal. Then Xander Quentin, a big British bloke who was former SAS and Kenji's best friend. Xander had recently fallen in love with a woman in Florida and was now splitting his time between the East and West Coasts. He had just finished an assignment in New York and was taking time off over the holidays to spend with Obie, his girlfriend.

Last, but certainly not least, there was Van Price. He wasn't that tall, but he was solid. All muscle from the tip of his bald head to his broad shoulders with the tattooed angel wings that peeked out from under his collar.

"We've got a new client. Should be a nine-to-five gig and will be running through the holidays and into January," Van said as he came in. "I know I promised some of you time off, so…"

"I'll do it," Kenji said.

"Mate, I thought you were coming to Florida with me," Xander said as he turned to him. His best friend looked hurt.

Kenji clapped him on the shoulder. "It's more important you go."

Xander bro-hugged him. "Yeah. Thanks for that."

"Depending on where it is, I could do it. Nicholas will be working until Christmas Eve," Luna said.

"I've got this," Kenji said. He needed to be busy, more than anyone else. "Unless I'm not right for the job?"

He looked over at Van, who just gave him that slow smile of his. "You're perfect for it. A local attorney was shot while meeting an informant about a case of potential art theft they're investigating, and her firm wants a bodyguard."

Cakewalk.

"Who is it?"

"Lee? You got the presentation ready?" Van asked.

Lee's fingers moved over the keyboard of the laptop she took everywhere with her, and the presentation flashed up on the screen at the end of the boardroom. But he wasn't listening or paying attention once the photo of the client was shown.

Daphne Amana.

Well, screw him. Of course he'd volunteer to protect the one woman he was pretty damned sure didn't want to see him again. He couldn't tear his eyes away from the screen. She'd matured, of course. It had been nearly twelve years since he'd told her *see ya* and broken up with her.

Her deep brown eyes sparkled with intelligence, and her face was still gorgeous, with high cheekbones and a full mouth. She had long black hair and tanned skin. In the corporate photo, she wore a suit that had been tailored to fit her shape in a way that immediately stirred regrets in him about how he'd walked away from her.

He'd done it because family hadn't been in his plans at twenty-three. He'd known that he wanted the most dangerous assignments the CIA had to offer, and having Daphne in his life would have been a liability. So he'd ended it, never expecting to see her again.

But here she was. Doing the good work she'd always wanted to do and putting herself in danger.

"Kenji?"

"Huh?"

"Mate, you okay?" Xander asked.

No way was he bringing up Daphne. He was the best man to keep her safe. Something Van might not agree with if he was aware of their past.

"Yeah," he said, shaking his head. "I'm good. When does the gig start?"

"Today. Head over to their offices, where you'll meet her and assess the situation," Van said.

"Cool."

The meeting went on with everyone updating the team on their current assignments or being briefed for the next one, but his attention was on his phone, where Lee had sent the case file. Daphne Amana. He wasn't sure this assignment was going to be the distraction he'd wanted. But he couldn't step away now.

Kenji walked back to the elevator to get ready for his assignment. Like there was a way to get ready to see the one woman he'd never really forgotten. He'd had moments when he'd thought of her. Had googled her late at night when he wasn't working or playing *Halo* against Xander online. Despite that, he'd never reached out.

When he walked down the hall, he noticed someone had put Christmas wreaths on his and Xander's doors. Kenji stood there staring at the display of holiday cheer. Christmas was going to be all around him. There was no way around it. At this time of year, he had to just grit his teeth and get through it. Normally work was a good distraction, and one time when X had been off the same time as he was, they'd gone to Aruba, rented a house, and gotten drunk and laid by some gorgeous women at their resort for ten days.

It had been perfect. No sign of Christmas or thoughts of exes or parents—the ones who were around and the one who hadn't ever tried to see him.

He rubbed back of his neck and used the security app on his phone to open the door as he heard the elevator opening. As close as he and X were, he didn't want to talk about Daphne or Christmas.

"Hold up, Kenji," Xander called as he got off the elevator.

"Yeah?"

"Hmm, well, I don't want to overstep, but is something up with you?"

They normally didn't do the intense emotional shit unless they'd both been drinking, when they could pretend that neither of them would remember it. So Kenji knew he must be showing signs of weakness. This was the one time when he shouldn't be.

"Dude," he said. Then realized that he was about to open up big-time, and neither of them wanted that. Also he didn't want to burst X's love bubble. He shook his head and opened his apartment door. He and Xander were the only two with apartments on this floor.

Xander put his hand on Kenji's shoulder and squeezed it. "I'm here if you need anything. Obie's working hard studying for finals, so I'm sort of at loose ends because Van didn't want me to get stuck out on assignment. But..."

Kenji turned and looked at the man who was more like a brother to him than just a friend. Xander was a lot like him. Work kept them grounded. True, Xander had his fiancée now, but that hadn't changed who he was at his core.

"I will. But like Van said, it should be a breeze," Kenji said. Hoping Xander bought it.

His friend just raised both eyebrows. "'Kay, but if it's not, I'm here."

"Thanks."

Chapter 2

Daphne's first day back in the office was three days later, and she was met with lots of sympathy. Carl already had visited her in the hospital and learned she'd been meeting an informant, so he had insisted that they were hiring her a bodyguard. That felt extreme. She was capable of taking care of herself, which she'd pointed out. It was her quick thinking that had kept her alive, even if going at all had been a dangerous idea. But Carl had just looked at her shoulder with a grimace, which was in a sling since the bullet had passed through. She was on strong pain medication, which she was trying to wean herself from because it made her mind foggy.

She'd had a quick look in the burlap sack and immediately recognized it as a censer, but hadn't been left alone long enough to check it against the museum's list of missing items.

She hadn't had a chance to examine the burlap bag and had hoped to today, but she had to be in court at ten and now was going to have a bodyguard with her. Daphne'd tried to argue against it, but Carl had threatened to pull her from the case unless she agreed. So she'd acquiesced.

Carl was fifty-eight but looked more like forty something. His hair had been red when she'd started working for him but now seemed more blond as he'd aged. He had laugh lines around his eyes and was easy to smile and joke with around his staff. Contrasting with his jovial personality, he was surprisingly tall, with broad shoulders and a square jaw. She knew from their annual picnic that he was a pretty decent beach volleyball player. The company game was always highly contested due to the competitive natural of most lawyers.

Back in the day, when he'd still been taking cases to court, he was legendary for his laid-back attitude and easy wit. It was said he could lull the opponent into believing the case would be an easy win. He was also known for charming judges and juries. To be honest, Daphne looked up to Carl and had tried to pick up as many tips from him as she could while she'd been working with him.

He was the main reason she'd accepted the job at Mitchell and Partners. Carl had a strong core of integrity, and his morals were impeccable. He didn't take a case based on how much money a client had or if it would be an easy win the way some firms did. Carl had told every one of his attorneys to only take a case if they were passionate about it.

Which Daphne was about this one. There should never be a world where a country could invade another and just take what they wanted and claim it for their own. There were still so many scars left from the brand of colonialism that scattered these artifacts across the globe. So many wrongs yet to be made right. Daphne worked hard to restore the treasures stolen in those past and forgotten crimes.

She was still ticked about it—her case and her bodyguard—when Kenji Wada walked into her boss's office. Turning away from him to look out the floor-to-ceiling glass windows that lined Carl's corner office, she tried to process this without giving anything away.

Kenji.

He hadn't changed at all based on that one glimpse of him in a fitted black suit, white shirt, skinny tie. He still had that angled jaw and that swoop of black hair that fell over his left eye. The rest of his hair was kept short and neat in the back and on the sides.

"Daphne, this is the bodyguard we've hired from Price Security, Kenji Wada."

She stepped forward, putting on her corporate smile and holding out her right hand. "Nice to see you again."

She wasn't going to pretend they didn't know each other. And as Kenji put his sunglasses in the breast pocket of his suit jacket and took her hand, a shiver of sensual awareness went up her arm and straight to her core. He was still that sexy, hot guy that she'd never really forgotten. But she wasn't twenty-three anymore. Her life was about a lot more than a guy.

"Same."

"Great, you two know each other?"

"Yes, we were in college together," Daphne said.

"Perfect. Then there won't be any awkwardness. I'll let you two get acquainted in your office. Are you still going to court this morning, or are you sending one of your assistants?"

"I'm going. The museum is trying to use my injury

as a reason to delay the evidence hearing, and I'm not letting that happen," she said.

"Of course you aren't," Carl said with a note of pride in his voice.

Daphne walked out of his office, very aware of Kenji following behind her down the hall. When she got to her own office, her assistant wasn't at her desk, but Daphne had asked for some files to be pulled from the archive and suspected that Rae was still down there. Dealing with Kenji alone couldn't be any worse than getting shot. Maybe. She started to go into her office, but Kenji stopped her with his hand on her arm.

She glanced down at the hand and then up into his dark eyes. "Excuse me."

"I have to check the room before you go into it. Stand in the doorway where I can see you," he said as he opened the door and walked into her office, keeping his eye on her as he swept the room.

"This is ridiculous."

"Says the woman with the shoulder injury."

He turned away, and she had to fight the childish urge to give him the finger. She'd gotten in over her head. Knew it even before she'd stepped out of her car to come into work, but this felt…like a punishment. She needed the freedom to go back to the alley and see if more clues had been left behind there.

No one cared about her case as much as she did. It didn't help matters that she was a control freak and really only trusted herself to get things done properly. Not that that belief was remotely true. These cases were the result of a lot of teamwork and expertise, not just her own.

She also really wanted to examine whatever was in the burlap bag and check the inventory of missing items the museum had sent over to see if it was on the list. Having Kenji around would make that nearly impossible. But if she did it right she could go on her own and he'd be close by if she got into trouble...not that she would.

"I'm pretty sure no one is waiting in my own office," she said, leaning against the doorjamb as she watched Kenji move. There had always been a fluidity to his movements. It was hard to keep her eyes off his body and to maintain the façade that she was mad he was making her wait.

The reasons for her anger at him were more than a decade old and very personal. She'd already decided that he was in the past, so she wasn't going to ask him why he'd dumped her the way he had. Even if it would be the perfect time for some karmic retribution. There had been no fights, no waning of the passion between them. Nothing to indicate he'd decided to move on. Just an *I don't think we should see each other anymore* before he packed his things and moved out of their shared apartment.

"I'm going to need to move your desk to that corner, away from the door and window," he said.

"Fine. Do you want some help?"

"I don't think you should strain your shoulder," he said.

She poked her head out of the office and saw one of her new paralegals, Alan Field, walking toward the office. "Can you come help move my desk?"

"Sure." He assisted Kenji with the task. "Glad you're

back. I have some more notes for this morning. I can come back later to discuss them."

"No. Stay. He's just my bodyguard," she said.

Alan paused for a moment then just shrugged. "Okay. Want a coffee before we start?" Alan asked.

"Please. Kenji?"

"Nothing for me," he replied.

Alan left, and she moved into her office. She put her laptop on the work surface while Kenji checked that the plugs were still all working. As she sat down, she wanted to ask him a million questions, but he was treating her like she was a stranger. Probably as he treated all of his clients. Something that she was determined to do, too. She wasn't going to be the one to ask why he'd waited so long to come back into her life.

Luckily she had a case that was way more interesting than Kenji Wada. Or at least, that was what she was going to tell herself. It was only the fact that she'd been shot at in a dark alley that had brought him back into her life. He probably didn't want to be here or see her again.

When Alan came back with Pam, her legal secretary, Kenji stopped them.

"What are you doing?" Daphne asked.

"My job. I need to take photos of everyone who comes into contact with you."

"How is taking photos of my staff your job?" she demanded.

"Someone tried to kill you. I need to rule out suspects and accomplices," he said, keeping it short and succinct.

"Will you back down on this?" she asked, knowing she only had so much energy. This fight wasn't worth it if she couldn't win.

"No."

"Fine, go on with it," she said. "Alan, do you mind being first?"

"Not at all."

The paralegal was young, in his late twenties, and had been on her team only a short time, but he had proved reliable and valuable. He had dark blond hair that he wore short but shaggy on the top, and he always wore a collared shirt and a pair of khaki trousers. Because it was December, he'd started wearing either a hunter green sweater or a Christmas-red one over the shirts.

He also had a short nose and full mouth. He often looked like he was brooding, but Daphne had realized it was just his face. Carl called him the moody one. But Alan's attitude was upbeat and cheery. He'd been the one to bring a Christmas tree into the office, and the day she'd been shot, he'd brought some frosted sugar cookies in the shape of Santa's head in as a treat for them all.

When Kenji asked him to stand against the wall to take his photo, Alan straightened his collar and then looked directly at Kenji. While others might have seemed nervous or unsure, Alan just looked at Kenji as if daring the other man to find something in his background that was less than spotless, which made Daphne want to smile.

But she didn't. The reason he was here was because anyone could be a suspect in her shooting. Kenji as a bodyguard was deadly serious, and she knew that he'd keep her safe, even if some of his methods were a bit extreme.

"If that's all," Alan said to Kenji, who just nodded

and turned to the next person on her team. A line had begun forming outside of her door.

Alan came over to her with that intense expression still on his face. "Daphne, we had pushback from the courts on our request for financial data from the museum. I'm going to spend the morning going through precedent and seeing what I can find. Unless you need me on something else."

"No, that's good. Thanks, Alan."

He nodded and turned away.

She watched him leave and then noticed her legal secretary, Pam Beale, was next. Pam had been with Daphne since she'd come to Mitchell and Partners, starting three months before Daphne herself had been hired, and they'd worked together ever since.

Pam had shoulder-length reddish-brown hair that curled around her heart shaped face. She stood against the office wall, clearly not sure if she was meant to smile or not, her mouth moving in an awkward grin and then quickly dropping back flat.

"You can smile. It's not a driver's license photo, right, Kenji?" Daphne said.

"Yes, smiling is fine…unless you have a booking photo on your record already," Kenji said.

Pam looked horrified. "No. Of course not. I'm not someone who breaks rules."

"He's joking."

Kenji glanced over at Daphne. She just raised both eyebrows at him. As soon as he was done with this, they were going to have a little talk. Being her bodyguard meant he should adapt to her workplace. Not the other way around.

"I am," he agreed. "I'm sure you are a law-abiding citizen."

"Mostly," Pam said worriedly.

Which worried Daphne in turn. "Have you ever broken the law?"

"In eighth grade, I kept a book from my school library, and I still have it at home," Pam said.

Which relieved Daphne. That wasn't a serious crime. "What book?"

"*Forever...* by Judy Blume. My mom wouldn't let me buy it," Pam said. "I did donate to the school library after college."

"I'm not surprised to hear that." Daphne said, holding back a chuckle. "When you get back to your desk, can you please send an email to Marjorie? Let her know that I will be going to the museum tomorrow to compile a list of what they have in their inventory."

"Of course," she said before she left Daphne's office.

Daphne had changed so much, and Kenji didn't allow himself to be distracted by those changes. Instead he focused on the job. Moving her desk was a temporary solution to securing her personal space, but she had people in and out of her office most of the morning. He couldn't do more to protect her until they were alone. Meanwhile, Kenji sent the names and photos of each person who entered to Lee to run a background check on.

She seemed tired and probably in pain, as she'd refused to take her pain medication when her legal secretary, Pam, had reminded her it was time. Was this case personal for her? Was that why she was being so stubborn? He decided he'd do some research into that tonight.

This close, she smelled good, like summer flowers and a hint of spice. Her eyes were dark as she watched him taking photographs, and as always, mysterious. He had never been able to tell what she was thinking. Except when she'd been lying under him after they'd made love.

Then she had relaxed, and he'd seen that wave of love and vulnerability on her face. It had scared him, he admitted, to know that another person cared for him that much. He shook his head to dislodge the thought. Nothing scared him anymore. Nothing.

"I'm done," Kenji said when he'd taken the last photo.

"Great. You need to stop being so brusque. One of the department assistants apparently had an anxiety attack after you took her photo."

"I'd think keeping you safe would be everyone's number one priority."

"Just be nice," she said, turning on her heel and walking back to her desk, where more of staff waited.

Kenji sent more information to Lee. He also pulled Pam to one side and asked her to find a space with no windows for Daphne to use until they found out who had shot her. The other woman agreed. While Daphne went to a meeting with the other attorneys on the Hazelton-Measham collection case, Pam would have Daphne's office moved to the new location.

Daphne wasn't too happy about that as they walked down the hall to the conference room for her meeting. "I understand you're trying to keep me safe, but I would appreciate if you spoke to me next time before having my office moved."

"You have more important things on your mind, and this move is necessary. So an argument with me would have cost you time away from your case and wouldn't have changed the outcome," he pointed out.

She almost smiled. He saw the hint of it in the way the side of her mouth twitched. "Fine."

She started to enter the conference room, but he stopped her. She sighed and leaned against the door, crossing her arms over her middle. "Stay here, right?"

He nodded, trying not to be affected by her full presence. It wasn't just that he was attracted to her—that had been the case since the moment he'd first seen her years ago. It was that he understood her frustration. She was strong and capable, so having someone else direct her moves had to be annoying for her. But Kenji took his job seriously, and he wasn't going to let anything bad happen. Especially to Daphne.

He opened the door and scanned the room from the doorway so that he was next to Daphne. The room was empty of people, with one long table in the middle and chairs on either side. There was a wall of floor-to-ceiling windows, which he'd expected. The room had only one entrance, but was window heavy like most office buildings.

"You should sit here," he said, pointing to the location that he deemed safest and easiest for him to protect. It was at the end of the room with walls on two sides, so that Kenji could see Daphne and the door and watch the windows as well. He couldn't rule out a sniper, even on a higher floor.

"Thanks," she said sarcastically, but then shook her head. "I appreciate what you are doing. I'm just on edge."

"I can tell," he said. "Is this case personal?"

"As much as any of them are. I just hate the sense of entitlement that comes from taking items that have meaning to someone and keeping them for yourself."

"You always did have a thing about stealing," he said.

"Everyone should. If it's not yours, don't touch it," she reminded him.

He smiled then. He had never taken the time to find out why that was a hot-button issue for her. Not that he condoned stealing, but growing up, there were times when he'd been poor enough to contemplate stealing food so that he and his mom would be able to eat. He knew she'd gone hungry to make sure he had meals.

"In a world where things are so uneven, sometimes thievery is a necessity."

"Agreed, but not in this case," she said.

"Can you share the details?" he asked her.

"Maybe later," she said as the door opened.

Two men and a woman walked in, followed by Alan, the paralegal he'd met earlier, and Pam.

"It is so good to see you today," the oldest man said. "We weren't expecting you back in the office so soon."

Kenji lifted his phone to quickly take photos of the new faces. Daphne reached out to stop him, but he stepped aside.

"Forgive the intrusion," Kenji said. "But I need to make sure Daphne stays safe."

"Of course," the man said.

Daphne introduced everyone as he took photos,

which he then sent directly to Lee. The oldest man was
Pierce Lauder, the museum director. He looked to be
in his early fifties and had probably lived in LA all his
life as he was fit and tan and looked really good for his
age. The other man was his attorney, Ben Cross, and the
woman was their paralegal, Lori. No last name given.
But Lee would discover that soon enough.

The meeting started, and Kenji leaned against the
corner wall, watching the room and the occupants. He
felt the underlying tension in the museum director and
suspected the man must be hiding something.

Chapter 3

The pain in Daphne's shoulder was unrelenting, but she was determined to get through the day before she took any more medicine. She needed to be clear-minded for this meeting. Pierce and Ben were being very solicitous, but she couldn't help feeling like they saw her injury as an opportunity to force this case into the new year.

Ben was about ten years older than she was. He'd slowed down the number of cases he took since he'd made partner. His face was slightly fuller with age, but he still had a full head of medium-brown hair that he wore short and spiky. Ben favored dark suits and brightly colored ties.

He was a tough opponent in the courtroom. He seemed to remember every other time he'd been up against her, and he would use anything—especially mistakes she'd made previously—to his advantage. He kept her on her toes normally.

Today, when she was tired and her shoulder still ached, hearing him offer to delay felt like a ploy. She met his blue-green eyes and tried to stare him down to see if he was rattled. Perhaps her injury scared him. He just gave her that tight fake smile that they all seemed to have picked up after years of working in this business as he waited for her answer.

He was from Boston, and rumor had it he'd worked in the district attorney's office before coming to the West Coast. He'd started work at Lawson, Cross and Parker when it was only Lawson and Parker. He'd been hungry to move up, which she could relate to.

That was why she'd taken the appointment at The Hague clerking as one of her first jobs. She'd always had a clear path of where her career would take her. This case was an important next step.

She'd become a lawyer to make the world a more just place, as trite as that might sound. But a case like this one, returning items that had been stolen during colonization, was something that Daphne was passionate about.

So anything that wasn't getting her closer to standing in front of the judge and making her case wasn't on the table, as far as she was concerned.

His client, the Los Angeles Museum of Foreign Cultures, was fighting hard to hold on to the pieces in its collection because they made up the backbone of the museum, which was opened in 1985 after the sale of the Hazelton-Measham collection. Jonathon's descendant, Henry Hazelton-Measham, had donated the entire collection to the museum, and it had drawn a large crowd of people and lots of attention in the press.

Pierce Lauder had a sophisticated look about him, almost like he'd been raised around fine art. She'd had a conversation with Marjorie about him, and she'd mentioned that he was well-traveled and had been to see her at her offices in Amba Mariam more than once.

He understood the global significance of his collection and returning it to Ethiopia, at least from what he said. He wore a tailored suit and always had a tie on when Daphne met with him. His salt-and-pepper hair was cut short and stylish. He always was well put together and his aftershave was subtle, and he had an East Coast accent similar to her mother's. Maybe that was why Daphne always got her back up when he spoke to her. There was something about Lauder that reminded her of her mom and the constant disapproval that she'd always showed toward Daphne.

The deputy director of the museum, Dan Jones, wasn't with Pierce today. The other man was more laid back and easier to handle. If she was being honest, Dan was a lot more malleable. Whenever she called and spoke to Dan, it was a matter of hours before she received the information she requested. With Pierce it could be weeks or months.

There was no way she was agreeing to any delay in this case if Pierce suggested it.

Pierce looked to be about fifteen years older than Daphne was, and she knew that his family had been running the museum since it had opened. It was easy to see that the museum's reputation was closely tied to Lauder's own, or at least, it was in his eyes.

He had other things going on managing his family's money and charitable organizations. But the museum seemed to be at the top of his priority list.

Daphne thought that should have made the other man more willing to work with her and her client. There would be a lot of goodwill generated toward the museum by returning the items to their rightful owners.

Pierce had consistently implied that the collection was safer in Los Angeles. As if the items would be damaged if transferred back to their home country. Something Daphne was determined to avoid at all costs.

"When I heard you'd been shot, my first thought was of concern for you, but also that we should push back the court date and give you time to recover," Ben said.

"I agree with Ben. There's no rush in moving this forward," Pierce seconded. "We can wait until January."

"There is a rush for my client. They have been waiting a long time to bring these important pieces from the Ethiopian Orthodox Church home. You also have ceremonial pieces that they are hopeful to have recovered for Easter next year. I do appreciate your concern for my health, but I don't need a delay," Daphne said. Pam, who sat next to her, smiled.

Her team supported moving ahead with the case. She wasn't going to allow any delays now that she had a piece from the museum. One that she still had to examine. That burlap bag told her something fishy was going on.

"We have already filed with the court to ask for a postponement."

"We will counter-file, insisting things go on as scheduled. To that end, I will be at the museum tomorrow morning at ten to examine the storerooms, as we agreed," Daphne said.

Pierce wrote something on the notepad in front of him, turning it so that Ben could read it. This wasn't the first case of this sort that she'd handled. Most of the time, discussions were enough to ensure that the items were returned to the country they were taken from.

But Pierce had stood his ground, which had forced this case into the court system. Daphne knew that there was more going on than just the museum wanting to keep their display.

To be fair, the exhibit was a rare one in this part of the world. Little was known about the Ethiopian Orthodox Church, and seeing the antiquities on display here was sharing that culture with a wider audience, but it wasn't the museum's culture to share. And Marjorie Wyman had insisted her country wanted their ritual headpieces and altar items retuned.

"I'm not sure I'll be available to show you around," Pierce said.

"That's fine. I have the inventory that Marjorie provided us as well as the records you shared during discovery. The archive numbers should match the boxes in your storeroom, and I need to confirm what items are still in the museum's possession and which ones are missing as you've indicated."

Ben cleared his throat. "The court has given you permission to do so, but we both know this shows a lack of trust in my client. He's been transparent about the items, which he could have listed as stolen. He's not hiding them in the archives."

Daphne wasn't too sure that was the case. It was odd to her that the missing items were ones that had no real pattern. They were all smaller items of the size that would fit in that burlap bag waiting in her shoulder bag back in her office. Some of them had significant monetary value. She hadn't been able to find a pattern in the items listed as missing.

"I never meant to imply that he did. I just need a thorough inventory of what the museum has. Also, several of the items were asked not to be displayed by the cultural minister because of their sacred nature. The tabots from Maqdala are not on public display, so I need to just ascertain their location and condition," Daphne said.

"Of course. As I said, we are happy to accommodate your visit. We do ask that it just be you and not your entire team," Ben said.

Kenji stirred from his position against the wall. "I will accompany Ms. Amana tomorrow."

He wasn't asking, Daphne thought.

"Of course, your safety is important to us," Ben said. "I hope you continue to feel better. I won't be at the museum tomorrow. I'm sure you'll send me your inventory when it's completed."

"Definitely," she said. "Thank you for coming to my offices today and for your good wishes on my health. I'll see you tomorrow, Pierce."

"Indeed."

The meeting ended and the others left the conference room, but Daphne stayed where she was. When she was alone with Kenji, she turned to him.

"What did you think?"

"Lauder isn't being entirely truthful with us. He was nervous, and whenever you weren't looking at him, he sort of glared at you."

"Yeah, he's not happy with me," she said, unable to help the smile on her face. He had been the museum director for over twenty years. From her research, she knew that he'd been successful in keeping most of the contested items in the museum on display and declaring the museum as the owner of them. This wasn't the first attempt at getting them returned. Very few of the exhibits were even on loan. Almost all of them were museum property, which was something that Pierce prided himself on.

"I can see that. The attorney respects you and seems frustrated with the case and maybe your determination."

"Probably. Plus, the last time we went up against each other in court, I won. So there is that," she said. "I'm not sure what I'm looking for, but I just feel like the museum is hiding something."

Kenji nodded. "Tomorrow will hopefully give you some answers."

"Hopefully. I do need a few minutes alone when we get back to my temporary office. Do you think once it's secure you could wait outside?"

She wanted to look into the burlap bag and find out what was in it. She needed to know if she was risking her life for a real clue that could help her find the missing items from the museum's inventory, or if she was just looking for danger where there was none.

"Sure."

Kenji led her back to the new office, which was actually an old storeroom. Daphne didn't mind the smaller space, though. Once she was alone, she gave herself a few minutes to silently cry because of the pain in her shoulder. Then, realizing she didn't have any more meetings for the day, she took her pain medication.

Why was she putting off opening the bag? Was she scared that it would be a stolen object, confirming her suspicions?

But she knew she was. Finally she put it on her desk, positioning her large shoulder bag so that it would block

anyone who entered from seeing what was in the burlap sack. She opened it carefully and tipped it until fell
out. It was a censer. She recognized it from examining
pictures of a similar one that was housed in the British
Museum and was also part of a contested collection.
This censer had a lid and was made of silver but was
smaller than the one in London.

Censers were used for burning incense during liturgical ceremonies. This one was engraved with serpen-
tine motifs, and the main container was engraved with
pairs of angels on all four sides.

She touched it carefully. It was exquisite, and she
quickly accessed the inventory list on her computer and
found that this censer was one of the missing items.

That was it. She had to go back to the alley where
she'd been shot. Needed to be sure there weren't more
bags like this or maybe some other clue she'd missed.
The only problem she saw was getting her bodyguard
to agree.

It took her all afternoon to figure out how to do it.
Kenji hadn't mentioned their past once, so when it was
time to leave, she took a deep breath and turned to him.

"How have you been?"

How had he been? Kenji didn't know where to start,
and wasn't even entirely sure what she was asking. She
was staring at him, and in this moment, he was very
aware that he was her bodyguard and that he probably
should clear up anything from the past to ensure this
job went more smoothly.

He shook his head, giving a small laugh. "I'm okay."

"You understand what I'm asking, Kenji. I want to

know what you've been up to since we last saw each other," she said.

"I don't think the hallway is a great place for that chat," he said.

"You're right about that. How about we go and get some coffee and talk? It might make the next few days easier."

"Okay," he said.

She started to lead the way, but he pulled her back. "Next to me or behind me."

"This is so hard. I'm not used to following anyone."

Of course she wasn't. As they got to the elevator, he checked the inside and then gestured for her to get on with him. "It is an adjustment. You seem…in less pain. Did you take your medicine?"

"I did," she said. "I'm not just being difficult about that. It clouds my mind, and like I said to you earlier, I suspect Pierce is hiding something."

"I'm glad you were able to take it," he said. He had nothing else to add about Lauder at this moment. He'd asked Lee to do one of her deep-dive background checks on everyone involved in the case. Lee had worked for a government agency on an elite task force. She'd been the computer geek assigned to the team—her words, not his. She was just really good at finding things on the internet that no one wanted found.

"So, I guess you can just follow me in your car," she said.

"Nope."

"Nope? Kenji—"

"I'm your bodyguard, Daphne. That means keeping you safe. I'll drive," he said. "You can pick the coffee shop."

She frowned at him. "I was planning to."

He wasn't going to defend his decision. He suspected she knew that, because although she didn't seem happy about it, she walked beside him and then got into his car when he opened the door.

His car was a special model that everyone at Price Security drove on jobs. It was bulletproof and had GPS tracking and a cache of weapons in the trunk to cover all eventualities. Kenji was used to driving it, so he knew the car like the back of his hand, which would prove useful if he needed to do any defensive driving.

"Where to?" he asked when he got in.

"You've changed a lot," she said instead of giving him an address.

"You have, too," he said.

She gave him the address and then sat back into the leather passenger seat as he drove to the coffee shop she'd selected. The traffic wasn't too bad this time of night, not that it was ever quiet in LA.

Zara's Brew wasn't a place that he was familiar with, so he was on guard as they exited the car and walked into the coffee shop. It was set up like a diner with a bar along one wall and booth tables that ran along the windowed front of the building, with two additional booths in the back. One was near the hallway that led to the bathrooms. The one in the corner would offer Kenji a clear view of the door and hallway.

He selected that table and directed Daphne to it. "What do you want? I'll get it."

"Decaf latte and a muffin," she said.

"What kind?" he asked. What he really wanted to know was when she'd switched to decaf. When they'd been dating she'd drank six cups a day and would hold out her mug in the morning asking for that first cup so she could face the day. Also, why this place? It was large and well-lit. Hard to protect from the inside if her shooter came back. The glass didn't look bulletproof. Which he guessed was a good thing. Maybe crime wasn't that high in this area.

"Whatever they have. I'm not choosy," she said.

He waited until she was seated with her back to the wall and then walked over to the counter to order. He got a black double espresso and then carried their drinks and her snack back to the table.

The booth was a bit of a problem. He wanted to sit next to her to block her from the main room, but he knew he needed to be across from her to see the hallway and front entrance. At least he was a really good shot, so there was a chance he could hit anyone who came at her.

For now, it would have to do. He was on his guard as she took a delicate sip of her latte and then looked up at him.

"So…"

Dammit. She wasn't going to let the past drop. He knew that she had a right to ask questions, and he didn't mind giving her answers. But that didn't mean he wanted to give them right now, when learning about her could rattle him and jeopardize their safety. However, he'd always done what was best for his client, and having Daphne trust him was paramount for her safety. That clearly meant she needed closure about their past.

Chapter 4

The interior of the coffee shop was all paneled light brown wood. It had graffiti art on the far wall that had different coffee sayings from movies. Somehow she'd missed that the last time she'd been here.

Well, to be honest, she hadn't exactly come in. Just glanced into the main restaurant, realizing that they'd been about to close after a late night in the office.

There were the standard espresso and coffee machines behind the counter. A glass cabinet that usually held pastries was empty this time of the day. But the chalkboard behind the counter advertised an array of fresh pastries and sandwiches.

Christmas music played low in the background. "White Christmas" came on, and she grimaced. If there was one song she hated, it was that one. She knew a lot of kids grew up dreaming of a snow-covered holiday, but for her, a snowy Christmas meant she'd be trapped inside with her mom.

Her mom wasn't abusive physically, but she'd been so emotionally withdrawn, and after several days, she would start to get mean toward Daphne. Then Daphne's father would suggest she go visit her grandparents until school started back. Which had been a welcome relief. They'd always been happy to see her and spoil her at their little condo in Boca Raton, Florida. It had been shitty flying alone as a kid just after Christmas, and the airports were a hassle, but when she'd got off the plane, Nanny and Poppa had been waiting.

The only Christmas she'd ever dreamed of was warm and sunny and spent lying on the beach. Sadly her grandparents were both gone, but luckily, in Los Angeles, Christmas wasn't snowy, and her dad came to spend the holiday with her some years. Not this year, though—he'd started dating Carmen, and they were going on a cruise since Daphne had thought her case would keep her busy until New Year's. Carmen was warm and kind and always talked to Daphne and not at her. Which was something she was getting used to. It was also a bit of a shock to see her father smiling as often as he did now.

She'd borne the brunt of her mother's ire, but she'd been unpleasant woman and hadn't made Daphne's dad's life easy either.

The song switched to Mariah Carey's "All I Want for Christmas Is You" just as Kenji had made his way back to her, and her heart beat a little bit faster. It would be a lot easier to deal with her ex back in her life if he'd somehow gotten less attractive to her.

Daphne had to tear her eyes from his lean, muscled frame. She'd seen him in action before. Would he still be as fit as he'd been back then? God, she hoped so. She wasn't sure if she was still in danger or not, but if she was going to be saddled with a bodyguard, he'd better be able to defend her.

How had her mom managed to hate someone as much as she'd hated Daphne? Not that she wanted to be anything like her mom, but it would make life a lot easier if she wasn't so hot for Kenji right now. Hating him would at least keep her focused.

She could tell that he wasn't really interested in telling her much about his past. Even when they first dated, he'd always been the strong, silent type. But he'd agreed to come, and she wanted to know what had happened to the boy-man she'd loved all those years ago. He was still hot as hell, but essentially a stranger. A stranger she was going to have in her back pocket for the foreseeable future. Getting to know him made sense. It would hopefully also give her some ideas on how to slip past her bodyguard when she needed to. More importantly, if he opened up a little, it would let her know if she could trust him with more information about the case.

"Kenji?"

He shrugged, looking down into his double espresso. He'd always been wired and drank massive amounts of caffeine. Interesting to see that hadn't changed.

"I don't know what to tell you."

"Start with the CIA. Did you stay with them?" she asked. They'd met when they'd both been recruited by the CIA after finishing their undergrad. It had been a sunny May day when she'd sat down in the testing room and first noticed him. Kenji had been serious and focused. They'd both gotten top marks, and by the end of the testing day, both had been asked to start in the recruitment program.

Daphne liked analytics, but some of the other training like sharpshooting and hand-to-hand combat wasn't up her alley. After a few weeks, she'd dropped out of the program, she'd gone to law school and eventually started dating Kenji. Until he'd come into their shared apartment six months later and broke up with her, packing his duffel bag and two boxes and leaving.

"Yeah, for almost ten years. I can't share the details of that," he said.

"Was it what you'd hoped it would be?" she asked.

He took a sip of his espresso. "Yeah. What about you? Ten years at this law firm?"

Interesting that he was deflecting, she thought. "Yes. Before that, I had a judicial clerkship at the International Court of Justice. I was offered a position in The Hague working as a judicial assistant, but I turned it down. I missed the US and wanted to come home."

He tipped his head to the side, studying her. She wondered what he was thinking, what he saw when he looked at her. She remembered those long, lazy summer days when they'd first gotten together. They'd spent hours with her reading a book for one of her courses, lying on Kenji's lap, while he played a first-person shooter video game. His hand would drift to her hair as he played.

Mentally she gave herself a hard smack. She needed to stay focused. She had a plan and intended to stick to it. Distract Kenji—not herself!

"What about you?" she asked. "Why did you leave the CIA?"

"I...don't want to sound arrogant, but I did everything I could with them. I'd had a lot of excitement and completed a lot of assignments that I hope made the world safer. But it was starting to feel like a job, and—don't laugh—a boring one at that," he said wryly.

She shook her head, smiling over at him. "One thing you hate is boredom."

"You know it. I was doing some freelance bodyguard and security assignments when Giovanni Price invited me to join his team. I said yes."

"Why?"

"I guess part of it was down to Van. I like the man, and I like the work I do for him. I'm not guessing if my skills are actually helping someone like I used to. I know they are. We have a tight, small team, and it suits me," he said.

She could tell that it did. There was something about him that was more relaxed than it had been back then. He was still tense in a way, but more measured. Kenji had always been on guard, watching everything and everyone. Daphne had believed then that nothing could catch him off guard, and she saw that he'd honed that energy into a solid strength now.

Which made her realize that in this whole time she'd been cataloging Kenji's changes, she was still no closer to figuring out how to get to the alleyway. More questions, she thought. There was a lot more she wanted to know about him.

"Where are you based?"

"LA. Though I do a lot of work overseas," he said. "What about you?"

"Same. I have a house in Bel Air." Being an international lawyer at Mitchell and Partners law firm paid pretty well and she had some family money she'd inherited.

"I know."

"You do? Have you been checking me out, Kenji?"

His face got serious for a moment. "Your address

came with the client profile. But I did look you up when I retired from the CIA."

Surprised, she wasn't sure how to respond to that. "Why didn't you contact me?"

"Your life seemed very focused, and I was proud of the success you'd achieved. I figured the last thing you needed was a man from your past."

"You mean a man who left without an explanation."

He shrugged, looking down at his espresso again. "Maybe."

"Why?"

Damn. She hadn't meant to ask that. To seem so hurt. But she had anyway, and she definitely wanted the answer now that the question was out there. It didn't matter that she'd told herself the personal questions were to distract him. Maybe she subconsciously chose to bring him here, to use this strategy, to ask that very question.

She'd never understood how he'd left. There had been no cooling of the passion, no fights or silences between the two of them. In fact, they'd been getting closer, and she'd thought that they would be partners for life. Until that day.

Her gut had never been so wrong before, and she hadn't really trusted it since.

"That doesn't matter. It won't change the past," he said.

"Of course not. But it might help me trust you," she said, using the same level tone she used when she had a difficult witness on the stand. "You're asking me to trust you with my life. Something that's not an easy ask. I thought I knew you, Kenji, and you walked away like I was nothing to you."

He put his hands on the table and leaned across it, closer to her. "You were never nothing to me."

Knowing she would probably bring this up, he'd rehearsed a few answers in his head, but the truth was, he couldn't tell her why he'd left. He'd been a young man with dreams that hadn't included the way she'd made him feel. He'd never really allowed himself to believe that he'd have a family one day. He'd had his mom, of course, but she'd passed away, and then he had no one. He'd always thought that remaining alone would make life easier. But it hadn't.

The truth of why he'd left the CIA was that he hadn't really liked the man he'd become when he'd worked for them. The longer he stayed, the more of his humanity he willingly gave away. He'd seen the worst side of people, and not just in one country or one people but in all of them. He had become jaded and lifeless.

Working for Price Security had given him back a little part of his soul. His friendships with the team, especially Xander, were strong, and he cared for them. Probably for the first time in his life, he felt like he had a family he could count on and a place where he belonged.

But he definitely wasn't going to tell her that.

"It didn't seem that way," she said. "I'm not going to lie to you. The way you left made me question everything I thought I knew about people."

Her words hurt him, because that hadn't been his intent. He had no way of really telling her that he'd been too excited for the possibility of saving the world. Being a hero, and proving to that faceless man who'd fathered him that he'd made a mistake when he'd walked out of Kenji's life. Stupid, but that was the truth.

As much as he'd cared for Daphne back then, there was no way he was giving up on that drive to prove himself. So talking about this now wasn't going to make her feel better about the past.

"I'm sorry."

"I know you are. You told me before you left. You never meant to hurt me," she reminded him.

"I didn't."

"I guess that's really all there is to say about the matter," she said. "I was surprised to see you today. Was there no one else at your company available?"

"I volunteered," he said.

"Oh. You're confusing me, Kenji…but then, you often did."

"I don't mean to. I was free, and Xander, the other bodyguard available, had planned to go to Florida to spend Christmas with his girlfriend."

"So you made sure he could. That's really nice of you," she said.

There was a distance in her voice that he probably deserved. He wished it was easier to convey that he still cared about her. He wanted to resist the attraction between them but still needed to know as much as he could about her life.

"Once I saw it was you, I wanted the assignment."

"Okay."

"Don't be like that," he said. He knew he hadn't made things better between them. But when had talking ever helped him? He was a man of action. Give him a tense situation and he shone. Guns and evasive maneuvers were easy to control, much easier than figuring out the right thing to say.

Daphne was the opposite. She used words as a weapon and a shield. He'd witnessed her doing just that during her meetings throughout the day. This was an uneven battle. Odd—he hadn't realized that they were adversaries until this moment. He'd thought they were getting reacquainted, but now he could admit that there was more going on here. She wasn't as blasé about him as she'd appeared all day.

He made too many assumptions where she was concerned. Maybe he should have let Xander take this client. Daphne was stirring things in him that he hadn't realized he still felt. God, he truly hated emotions. Why couldn't she just be an ex that he had fond memories of?

But he knew the answer. She'd never been just a woman from his past. He hadn't just looked her up when he'd retired. He'd spent a few weeks shadowing her and checking out her life. Looking for…some way back in. But this urbane, sophisticated woman really didn't need a man like him by her side, something that had been very clear to him.

Which was probably why he'd taken this job, looking for some kind of way out of the unsettling emotions she brought to life in him that he'd never been able to shake.

His phone buzzed in his pocket. Kenji glanced at his watch, which notified him that it was a call from Van. He couldn't ignore it.

"I have to take this call," he said.

"Feel free. I'm going to the bathroom," she said as he answered the call.

He nodded. He could see the hallway from his seat and assumed there wasn't a back exit.

"This is Wada."

"Kenji, my man, how's it going?" Van asked.

"Fine."

"Wanted to let you know that Lee found something but hasn't finished running it down. She wanted me to pass on to you to watch your back and not trust anyone at the law firm."

"Thanks. Anything else?"

"Not now."

"Bye."

He ended the call. A shiver of worry went down his spine. All day today, Daphne had been protective of the people who worked with her. The fact that Lee had something on one of them concerned him. Convincing Daphne to keep her guard up would be hard. She always led with her emotions.

That was part of why he'd left. He hadn't wanted to hurt her with the reality of how people were. She trusted everyone. Life had proven to him that people never lived up to that trust. It had put Daphne at risk.

What was taking her so long?

He got up and walked toward the hall, noticing the emergency exit door.

Dammit.

Had someone been waiting for her?

This was why he shouldn't have been answering personal questions and letting his guard down. He wasn't going to lose Daphne. Not like this.

He pulled his weapon from his shoulder holster as he crept down the hall. He opened the unisex bathroom door, which wasn't locked, and confirmed that Daphne wasn't in there.

They he continued further down the hall, opening the emergency door, which didn't trigger an alarm. The alleyway was dark and full of shadows. He glanced both ways, unable to see Daphne.

Daphne took a deep breath before she stepped out into the alley. The conversation with Kenji had been a double-edged sword, cutting both ways. What had she expected? Relationships had never been easy for her, and the one with Kenji had been more complicated than she should have ever allowed it to be.

But this case had brought him back into her life, and the sooner she had the information she needed on the missing artifacts, the sooner she could put this case before the judge and get him back out of her life.

No more asking personal questions.

As if she would be able to keep from wanting to know more about him and to possibly understand the flaw inside her that had caused him to leave. It wasn't like she was hopelessly flawed in other things. In her work, she thrived. She was sought-after by big clients and countries who knew she'd get justice for them.

Which was what she was determined to do for Marjorie Wyman and her country. Kenji would be dealt with later.

Carefully she opened the door and stepped out into the alleyway. It was a bit earlier than when she'd been here the last time but still shadowy and dark as the nights grew longer. Taking her phone from her pocket, she turned on the flashlight function and stooped down to where she'd found the burlap bag.

She noticed blood spatter on the ground. Hers? She remembered hitting her head on the edge of the large dumpster and seeing some dark blood spatter stains from the bullet that had gone through her shoulder on both the dumpster and the ground.

Moving slowly and being very careful to look at every possible place, she noticed more dark spots on the ground, closer to where the bag had been tucked. Daphne took a night mode photo of the ground with her phone to examine later.

It was growing even darker, and she'd taken another dose of her pain medicine before she'd left work, so her mind wasn't as sharp as it usually was. Maybe that explained her asking Kenji why he'd left her. She shoved that thought out of her head.

She heard something—or someone—at the end of the alley and flicked off the flashlight as she crept around the corner of the dumpster, moving back against the wall.

Holding her breath, she waited to see who was coming. Maybe the person she'd been about to meet was coming back? Whoever had dropped the burlap bag with the censer in it wasn't going to just leave it abandoned here. Not for long. That censer was valuable, and unless Mr. Lauder was going to report it as missing—which he hadn't done so far—the museum was going to need it back in the collection by tomorrow when she came to examine the items.

She peeked around the edge of the dumpster but couldn't see anyone. Daphne stepped further away from the restaurant, focused on the end of the alley where the shot had come from the other night. And where she'd thought she'd heard something a few moments ago.

Her heart was racing, and she was scared, but also angry. Angry at herself for putting herself in danger again, but angry at Kenji for making her not trust him, forcing her hand to do this one on her own.

Doing things on her own was what she did, so she was used to it. But this time it might have been better if she'd been able to trust him and include him on this. Although she didn't really trust anyone except her clients.

Standing, she continued moving carefully as she got closer to the end of the alleyway, where she realized that there was a chain-link fence and no way out. They could have climbed out but would have had to wait until she wasn't looking in that direction. Had the person who shot her watched her on the ground? Had they hoped she'd bleed out before help arrived?

That actually creeped her out a little bit. Believing her assailant had shot her and run had been different than this. This meant he'd been close and hadn't finished her off. Had watched her and possibly had waited until the cops had arrived and then snuck away, as if basking in her suffering. Had she seen him that night and not noticed?

Also, it didn't escape her that she was referring to the assailant as *him*, but it could easily have been a woman. She'd been groggy when the cops arrived, finally feeling safe enough to let herself drift off. Had she missed something?

A hand came down on her good shoulder. She

screamed, hoping Kenji would hear her, and brought her knee up, hoping to hit the person behind her with a solid jab. But as she turned, she saw that thick fall of black bangs and those angled cheekbones.

Kenji.

"What are you doing out here?" he demanded, pushing her back against the wall and using his body as a shield.

"Never mind. I think I heard someone."

He pulled her down, pushing her toward the dumpster again. She was becoming really familiar with this part of the alley.

"Stay low and stay hidden."

He had his weapon secure in one hand as he moved away from her. He made a visual sweep of the area before he shifted down the alleyway, a short distance to the fence she'd noticed earlier, then came back.

"Get up. There's no one here now."

She struggled to stand, probably thanks to her meds and panic. Kenji offered his hand, which she reluctantly took. Once she was on her feet, he boxed her in again with the wall against her back. His hand came up to her jaw, and he turned her face until their eyes met.

"You might not like me, but this was stupid and dangerous. The threat to you is real."

"I know that."

"Sneaking off is a good way to get yourself killed. You're smarter than that. What were you doing?" he demanded.

She swallowed, and the adrenaline that had kept her fear at bay waned. She blinked a bunch of times to keep from crying—not that the danger was over. He clearly wanted to know what she was doing, but she wasn't ready to tell him. Not when it could put her case in further jeopardy.

So instead, she put her hand on his face and then leaned up, brushing her lips over his and kissing him.

Chapter 5

She tasted better than he remembered. And that was saying something, because when he wasn't working and he let himself remember, he always drifted back to the past and those moments in her arms. There was a familiarity to the way her body fit against his. He held her closer because she'd scared him running off like that, and for the first time on the job, he was very afraid he might not be able to keep her safe.

He deepened the kiss. Because it was Daphne, and he wanted even a small taste of the passion that had always sizzled between them, but then he broke it off as his body started to relax. He stayed vigilant though they were still in unguarded surroundings. The smell of the dumpster next to them was a reminder that he was on the job.

That his client wasn't safe and had done something stupid and risky. He wouldn't compound the problem by letting his hormones take over. Careful of her injured shoulder, fighting to keep his body under control, he put his arm around her and led her back to the emergency entrance of the coffee shop. The door wasn't locked from the outside.

Something he should have checked earlier, but he hadn't anticipated trouble here. Rookie mistake.

Once they were inside, he pulled the door closed and led her out of the coffee shop and back to his car. She was shaking and visibly pale as he came around and got into the car next to her.

"Daphne—"

"I'm sorry. I really didn't think this through. Any of it," she said.

"Tell me what you were doing out there," he demanded. Trying to tell himself she was safe and that he wouldn't fuck up again, but he doubted it. Had his twenty-three-year-old self known this? Had he simply forgotten the effect being around Daphne had on him?

"Well, you know I was meant to meet an informant the other night when I got shot."

He kept his level stare on her, just raised his eyebrows, waiting for her to go on.

"It happened in the alley behind this coffee shop," she said.

"You should have mentioned that," he told her.

"I know." She rubbed her forehead with her injured arm and he saw her fail to hold back a wince.

He knew she was in pain, and he should go harder on her about this. She could have gotten herself killed by running off. She needed to start thinking of the consequences. "It's dangerous for you right now. I'm here to protect you. Not judge you. If you needed to go back for some personal reason, that's fine. Let me check it out and keep you safe."

She nodded. "There's more, but I think I should explain it when we are back at my place."

"Sure," he said. He wasn't certain of what else she had to tell him, but right now, he wanted to get away from this street and the scare they'd both had. He'd gotten lucky that no one had been waiting for her. They both had been lucky.

He followed her directions and drove to her place. The radio quietly played as he navigated the streets of LA, and he heard the first notes of "Thrift Shop" by Macklemore. A throwback. He glanced over at Daphne. A smile played around her lips. This song had been playing on repeat at lunch in the cafeteria when they'd first started hanging out. Even before they'd hooked up, she'd called it their song.

She reached over and turned the volume up, starting to sing along. He sang with her. It was a safe release of tension for them.

Letting someone else watch over her wasn't the solution. He was going to have to man up and put his feelings for her aside. Except when she laughed as the song ended and gave him that soft look, similar to the one on her face when she'd kissed him, he knew that wasn't going to be easy.

He pulled into the drive of her house. "This is a nice place."

"Thanks. I worked hard for it. My dad thinks it's too big for one woman, but I like it."

He had never met her parents. She'd never mentioned them when they were together, and this sudden realization reminded him of how little they actually knew each other. They'd been so young that love and sex had seemed like it would be enough, and when he'd felt the pull of the excitement of being an elite agent for the CIA, he'd left before they could go deeper.

"Never mind what he said. You get to choose how you spend your money."

It was something his mom had said once when he'd felt guilty about buying a new game for his Game Boy. He'd promised to return it so they could use the money to pay for food. She told him it wasn't his responsibility to pay for food for them. Something he hadn't agreed with her on, yet she'd wanted him to have a childhood and not be her mini-man all the time. But that was the past, and he was here with the only other woman he'd ever allowed himself to care for. And she still hadn't told him about everything going on. He needed to rectify that before she pulled him in even further.

"Let's go in so you can tell me *everything*," he said.

"Okay. You said you wouldn't judge," she reminded him as they walked up the paved path to her front door, which was dark.

"You should have a security light that comes on, or leave on the front light if you're coming back late," he said to her.

"I always do."

He stepped around her and moved closer to the entrance, catching that the front door was slightly ajar.

"Go get in the car, lock the doors and call 911."

"What are you doing?"

"Making sure there's no one still inside," he said. "Go."

His adrenaline was pumping, and he was almost hoping there was someone in the house so he could have a fight or at least chase them. He watched Daphne as she went back to the car and waited until she was inside with the doors locked. The car was bulletproof, and unless someone fired at it with multiple automatic weapons, she'd be safe in there until he got back.

Even knowing that Kenji could handle himself in any situation, Daphne was tense the entire time he was in the house. She called 911 and felt a bit foolish doing it again so soon. She'd never had to use the service, and now she was becoming a frequent user. Like did they have a stamp card—every fifth call to 911 got you a special mug? They dispatched police to her house and advised her to get Kenji out of the building and someplace safe.

That wasn't happening. She'd seen the look on his face when he'd realized someone might be inside. There was no making that man stand down, and she knew it in her bones.

Believing in his skills was one thing, but her heart was still pounding until he appeared back in the doorway and returned to his car. He unlocked it as he got close and slid into the driver's side. "It's empty, but someone rifled through your stuff."

"What?"

"Yeah, it's trashed. We'll wait for the cops so they can fill out their report. I need to call my boss and keep him up to date. You good?"

Good?

"No. I'm the opposite of good, Kenji. You scared the crap out of me in the alleyway, which I totally deserved, but still. I was hoping to get home and maybe have a relaxing bath and rest my shoulder after a long day. Instead, my home is…" Her voice cracked, and she stopped talking.

She sounded like she was losing it. She *was* losing

it, she thought. Totally had enough of this day. She was tired and achy and scared and—

Kenji pulled her gently into his arms. Her mind stopped running in circles as she put her head on his shoulder. The familiar scent of his aftershave and the warmth of his body were reassuring in a way that the strong, independent woman she was didn't want to admit, but she soaked up every second of it.

She let herself cry for a minute and then wiped her eyes and sat up. "Thank you."

"It's been a day, hasn't it? I'm sure seeing me wasn't what you were expecting. At least I knew I'd see you," he said.

"Yeah, that was unexpected. I didn't even know you were back in the States, much less in LA."

His face was stone cold, and she couldn't read his expression but she could tell that he was determined.

"Let me check in with my boss," he said again.

He was on his phone talking quietly, and she listened as he related everything that had happened when they got to her house. He left out the coffee shop and their alley encounter. Which she was grateful for. She was scared. Whoever had contacted her had either been setting her up or had been injured or killed and had left the item for her. She still had a lot to figure out.

She was tired, and the effects of her pain meds were wearing off. She really hadn't been kidding about wanting a bath and some time to think. Just to feel safe. Safety was something she'd taken for granted and shouldn't have.

Justice had always been the one thing she put her faith in, and this case was about righting an injustice that had been dragged out for too long. The spoils of colonialism weren't something she took lightly, and if she could continue to make a difference, she would.

She was lucky this was the first time that someone tried to fight back outside the courtroom.

"Okay. Bye," Kenji said.

He pocketed his phone, turning toward her. The play of light and shadows over his face made his cheekbones seem even sharper, and she regretted that she hadn't touched him more during that ill-advised kiss she'd initiated.

"Is there anything you are hiding?"

What? She had mentioned needing to talk to him, but she wondered for a moment if he knew about the small burlap bag in her big purse. God, she hoped not. She wanted to trust him. Had been hoping that she could share the burden of this item she'd found with someone so she could discuss it and figure out how to use it to find the other items missing from the inventory.

She was also very aware that she should have turned the bag over to the authorities days ago. Kenji might question her motives for not doing that.

"Hiding?"

"Don't be cagey. You are too direct to pull it off. You said you had more to tell me, and your house has been broken into…so I'm asking you again if there is anything I should know before the cops get here."

He was so calm about it. "I found something the night I was shot, and I haven't had a chance to disclose it yet."

"What is it?"

Red and blue lights flashed around the car before she

could answer. "Something related to my case. Nothing criminal."

And it wasn't, technically. She'd found the censer, and she definitely planned to turn it over to the cops... once she had a chance to document it. Holding on to it as long as she had might make the cops unhappy, but there was no inherent criminal activity.

"Okay. We'll talk when they leave. For right now, keep that to yourself," he said.

"I was planning to," she said wryly.

"Stay here until I've checked their badges."

Kenji gave her a side-eye look as he opened his door and met the cops. Once he was sure they were legit, Kenji asked her to get out. Together with the cops, they went into her house.

She let out a gasp when she saw the damage to it. Paintings had been ripped from the walls. Cushions had been knifed clean open and stuffing spilled out on the ground. Nothing had been left untouched in her entire home. But oddly, her jewelry had been left behind, and she had some pricey pieces that had been left to her by her paternal grandmother.

Officer Martinez and his partner were very thorough as they searched her house for intruders. Martinez was the lead, she guessed, and the one who talked to her. He was young, in his late twenties, and wore an LAPD uniform. He had kind brown eyes and kept apologizing for asking her questions about what was kept in each of the cabinets, drawers and jewelry boxes that had been turned over.

Daphne struggled to hold her emotions in. Her shoulder still ached, but she wasn't a woman known for crying. Not that there was anything wrong with women's tears. But right now she just wanted to power through her house. Trying to be objective wasn't as easy as she had hoped it might be.

"I know this is a lot. You can write up a detailed list of anything missing and bring it by the station in the next day or so," Martinez said, pocketing the notebook he'd been holding.

"I might do that," she said, but he kept moving into the other rooms of her house. "Is there a reason you're still checking the rooms?"

"Just being thorough. We already made our observations, but you might see something we missed. A detail that might help us find the criminals."

"Like what?"

"A threatening message or something that only you'd recognize," Officer Martinez said. "Sorry to be vague, but usually it's a know-it-when-you-see-it kind of thing."

Daphne understood where he was going with it. Her house was wrecked, and there was no way the cops would know what belonged and what didn't. If there was any clue in this mess, she wanted it in their hands so they could find who did this.

But after continuing through the other rooms, she soon realized there wasn't anything but her belongings treated like trash as they'd been dumped on the floor and trampled on.

"They were looking for something," Kenji said.

"Do you know what?" Officer Martinez asked Daphne.

"I'm not sure. I have two big cases right now, but all of the evidence and files for them are kept at my office," she said.

"It's clear someone believes you have something of value. Hiring a bodyguard was a good idea. Do you have a place to go that isn't widely associated with you?"

"No. I mean, my dad lives in New York," she said. "I can't leave the state right now. Not with my caseload. I'm not willing to be the reason why there is a further delay in this case."

"Of course. There is a concern with this second attack that you are being targeted by someone sympathetic to the defendants in your museum case.

"She will be relocating to Price Tower," Kenji said, and gave the cops the address. "You can reach her through me."

He also provided his contact details. The officers just took his word that she'd go with him. It was almost comical. She was going to because she wasn't an idiot, and putting herself at risk of murder just to stay in her home was ridiculous, but she was also used to making her own choices and decisions.

Irritated at him, and more than likely just at the situation in general, she wanted to lash out at someone. Instead, she found herself standing in the middle of her ruined living room, listening to Kenji talk to the cops.

Officer Martinez left Kenji and the other officer to come over to her. He gave her a kind smile. "It's okay to be overwhelmed. You've been through a lot."

"Thanks."

"You should take a few days off from work. Give us time to find out who broke into your place and shot you."

"Thank you, but I can't."

He reluctantly nodded. "I understand. Do you have the police report for the night you were shot?"

"I do. It's in my purse in the car. I can't remember the name of the officer I spoke to."

"That's understandable. Most people don't. We can get it when we all leave," Officer Martinez said. He turned toward his partner before looking back at her. "Sorry about your Christmas tree, by the way."

She glanced over at the prelit tree lying on its side on the floor. The decorations were shattered, and she'd tried not to look at the mess it had become this whole time. Since she'd been on her own, she attempted to create a kind of Christmas that worked for her every year. Something that would give her a chance to be happy on the holiday without flying to Florida. Cass, her best friend and a fellow lawyer at Mitchell and Partners, had come over with her husband on the Saturday after Thanksgiving this year, and they'd helped her decorate it.

Now it was smashed on the floor, and she was trying not to see that as an omen. But in her heart, she was a fatalist. She saw signs everywhere.

Kenji coming back into her life was certainly one. She'd put herself in a dangerous situation, so that much was on her, not fate. He was only here because of that. No matter what they'd discussed at the coffee shop. Nostalgia could only go so far.

Her life was…well, her *personal* life wasn't much different than this hot mess of her house. She tried to do things that would make that part of her life more normal, but it seemed the harder she tried, the more she failed.

"It's okay," she said, realizing she hadn't responded to Martinez lost in herself.

Then she saw one of the ornaments had rolled close to where she was standing, and she bent to pick it up.

Turning it over, she saw it was a tiny picture frame, one that had a photo of her and her dad. She tucked it into the pocket of her jacket.

"I've spoken to my boss, and he is going to send a team over to clean this up and restore everything," Kenji said.

"I didn't know the bodyguard service covered that," she said.

"It does this time," Kenji said.

"Is it your boss footing the bill or you?" she asked.

"Does it matter?" he countered.

"Kenji."

"It's taken care of. I've never been here before and I am… I don't like seeing your house this way. Having it cleaned won't make this memory go away, but the next time you are here, at least it will all be sorted out."

She reached into her pocket and ran her finger over the ornament that had the photo of her father in it. Kenji's offer was gracious. He seemed more understanding that she had expected.

"Thank you. Make sure to send me the bill."

"Sure," he said, but turned to talk to Martinez, who informed them they could leave the house whenever they were ready.

They walked to Kenji's car, and Daphne took out the incident report from the night she'd been shot and gave the information to Officer Martinez.

Chapter 6

Kenji and Daphne went back into the house after the officers left so she could pack a bag to take with her to Price Tower. She'd seemed like she was going to argue going with him, but he had simply pointed to her ransacked house, and she'd gone to get her suitcase and pack without a word.

"Before we go, let's talk," he said when she was done packing.

She sighed as she sat down on her bed. "I'm not sure how much you heard about my case today, but it involves some contested items from the former city of Maqdala that is now part of modern day Amba Mariam in Ethiopia. The items came to the Los Angeles Museum of Foreign Cultures through a bequest from the grandson of a solider who fought in the major battle of the city and took some items with him as spoils of war.

"The items had been on display in the museum until I filed a case in court to find out if the items legally belonged to the museum or to my client. Once that case was filed, the exhibit was pulled, and several items seem to have gone missing," she said.

"That sounds suspicious."

"Yeah, I know. But the director has insisted they haven't been stolen or moved. They are simply missing during an archival reshuffle. Yet he hasn't given us access, even though the court has compelled them to provide us with entrance to the archives."

She knitted her fingers together and looked down at her hands. It was obvious she was stalling, and he allowed himself to look at the fall of her long, straight black hair over her shoulder, where it partially covered her face. She was so beautiful to him. Then she looked up, and their eyes met.

"The other night, I got a message saying that someone had information regarding the missing items. I tried to get them to come to my office, but they wouldn't so I suggested we meet at Zara's Brew. They insisted we meet behind the coffee shop so they wouldn't be observed."

Kenji made a disapproving sound.

Daphne held her hand up. "I know. Dumb. Dangerous. But I needed a break in this case. Something that I could tie to the museum. So I went."

"And that person shot you?" he asked.

"No. No one was there, like I told the cops. I walked into the alley, and there was a shot. I dropped to the ground and hit my head, and when I turned, I saw…"

She stopped talking, pulled her purse toward her and opened it, taking out a burlap bag with a small logo on the bottom corner. He moved closer and immediately realized it was the logo of the Los Angeles Museum of Foreign Cultures.

"This. I put it into my purse as the cops and EMTs arrived and didn't have a chance to look in it until today," she said.

She opened the bag and carefully removed the silver object inside. Moving closer, he could see the delicate item was engraved. It smelled faintly of incense.

"What is it?"

"It's a censer and part of the tabot used in the Ethiopian Orthodox Church. It's an incense burner used during masses on high holy days."

"How does it tie to your case?" he asked.

She put the item back into the burlap bag and then slipped it into her purse. "It's one of the missing items on the list. I was hoping to find more clues tonight in the alleyway. Maybe something that would lead me to whomever contacted me. I want to talk to the person who left this behind."

"Did you find anything?" he asked, coming to sit down next to her.

"Some blood spatter stains, but those are probably mine. The biggest thing was that the shooter was at the end where that chain-link fence was. I think they stood there and watched me until the cops came," she said, shivering slightly as she did so.

He wanted to put his arm around her but waited because he knew she wasn't done talking.

"When we got here and I realized my house had been broken into… I think whoever shot me knows I have the censer and was trying to get it back. What I don't know is if they work for the museum or not."

"You can't keep this item," he said.

"I know. I need to return it, but I am also meant to go to the museum tomorrow, and I want to bring up this censer and see Lauder's reaction. He's been difficult, but it could just be pride and stubbornness making him that way."

Her plan made a kind of sense given the nature of her work. But the longer she had the censer, the more danger there was to her. "Do you mind if I bring my team in on this?"

"Why?"

"Lee is really good at using the dark web to get information. I think she'll be able to search for black market dealers who would buy or sell items like this. It might help you find a connection between the museum and this item."

She pressed her lips together and then gave a tight nod. "I'm not used to doing this kind of leg work for a case. Any help would be great."

"Good. Ready to go?"

"Maybe."

"Maybe?"

"We never finished our personal discussion."

"And we're not going to here. I need to get you someplace safe. You can relax, I can check in with my boss, and then we can talk if you still want to."

She didn't like it, but she didn't argue either. He was ready to leave her house. Van had promised to have a security team come and secure it after they left. He trusted his boss to help keep Daphne safe while he found the people who were after her.

The Price Security Tower was located in downtown Los Angeles on South Broadway. He took the interstate from Bel Air. The Tower was near the Eastern Columbia Building. The Price Tower was only ten floors high and had an underground parking garage. As they left the 10 and he spotted the Eastern Building, Kenji felt safer. They were almost home, and there was no place he'd rather be right now.

He had to think and start to piece together where the threat to Daphne was coming from. At least now he could do that in the modern building that had been his home since he'd retired from the agency.

The building was steel-reinforced concrete and clad in glossy turquoise terra-cotta trimmed in deep blue and gold to match the Eastern Building. Van had spent about an hour talking about it and its history with Luna's husband, Nick DeVere, during their last get-together. They both loved old Los Angeles, having grown up in the city. But compared to his friends, Kenji was a child of the world, having moved around whenever his mom lost a job and needed a new one. As an adult, his life had followed the same pattern. He'd never really sat in one spot. Instead he was used to moving on.

So, yeah. This place was home.

He glanced at Daphne. Her features were occasionally visible as they passed under the street lamps. She had her arms wrapped around her waist, and she'd changed into a pair of ripped jeans and a form-fitting pink sweater that had a rhinestone reindeer on it. Somewhere along the way, she'd pulled her hair back into a ponytail, and he noticed that she leaned her head against the window almost the whole time as he drove.

It had been a long, tough day for her. And it wasn't more than she could handle. He knew she'd be ready for whatever else this night threw at her. But he was moved that she felt comfortable enough with him to let her guard down for a few moments.

His gut clenched. He wanted to be the man she could be safe with, who would protect her from whatever came at her. She'd been shot at, her home had been burgled, and he wasn't sure what the next attack would be. Whatever it was, he would meet it.

But protecting her from himself...was that also something he needed to be concerned with? He hoped not, but it had been too long since he'd allowed his emotions to leak out like this. Hell, not since the last time he'd been with her.

Even this relocation could be a mistake.

"We're almost here," he said.

"Price Tower is nice," she said. "I didn't realize this is where you lived. You know, the courthouse isn't that far from here."

He did, because he'd sometimes gone down there on his days off to see if he could catch a glimpse of her until he recognized what he'd been doing. That had been years ago, and he hadn't gone back since. Now she was sitting in his car, watching him with those wide brown eyes, and everything masculine in him was satisfied. *Yes*, his primal self thought, *she's mine*. But she wasn't, not really. No one knew that more than he did.

Price Tower housed offices and apartments for the entire staff. It was not too far from Nicholas DeVere's building, which included his penthouse and the nightclub Madness. Kenji's apartment was his private domain, and he seldom had brought any of his clients back to the tower. Usually it was reserved for the team, a place for them to relax.

But he couldn't leave Daphne at her place; it was too big and open for him to protect her alone. Bringing her here was logical. Or at least, that was the story he was sticking with for the time being. Van hadn't raised any objection when Kenji had texted saying he was bringing her here.

"Before I take you to my place, let's put that censer in the safe. We can talk to Lee so she can run a search on the dark web," Kenji said, hitting the button for the fourth floor, which was where the safe and Lee's office were.

"Okay to putting it in the safe, but tomorrow, after we visit the museum, I'm going to report finding it to the cops," Daphne said. "I know you suggested doing this. I don't want to keep it long-term. It might cause the judge to look unfavorably on my client."

"Not a problem," Kenji said.

The elevator opened. They stepped out into the hallway, and the lights clicked on as they did so. A door at the end of the hallway opened, and Van and Lee came out. Both were dressed in jeans and black T-shirts. Kenji didn't know much about the pair. They weren't romantically involved—he did know that much—but both had worked together before, eventually getting soured on working for the government and thus starting their own company.

"Kenji, good to see you," Van said as he came forward. "Ms. Amana, I'm Giovanni Price, and this is Lee Oscar. You're in safe hands with Kenji and in the Tower."

"Thank you, Mr. Price," she said, offering him her hand, which Van took and shook.

"Call me Van."

Daphne nodded.

"We have an item for the safe, and we need you to find out how it came to be in an alleyway behind Zara's Brew the night that Daphne was shot."

"Sounds like my kind of puzzle," Lee said.

Van turned to lead the way back down the hall. They entered a room that was dark and had a wall of monitors on the far side. Lee's desk had four monitors on it and two keyboards. It also had the model of top-of-the-line gaming chair that Kenji was thinking about ordering for his place. He spent a massive amount of his down-time gaming.

Van flicked on a light as he led them to the table in the middle of the room. Daphne had left her suitcase in the hall, and she took off her shoulder bag. She hesitated, and he remembered that she was putting a lot of faith in all of them to handle this potentially stolen artifact.

"It's okay," he said. "We won't take possession of the item, and no one is breaking in to steal it."

"I can personally guarantee that," Van said. "What is the item?"

"It was marked as missing in an inventory from the Los Angeles Museum of Foreign Cultures, among a number of other pieces that have been contested by my client, the cultural minister for Amba Mariam. I only had a chance today to look in the bag that I found the night I was shot. I was surprised to see this item. I specifically asked Mr. Lauder if it had been stolen when I first took the case and noticed its value and the fact that it was missing, and he said no."

"So how'd the item get from the museum to the alleyway?" Van asked.

"Exactly. There are more missing items that might be out there," Daphne said. "Do you think you can help in any way?"

She turned to Lee for the last question. Lee leaned down to inspect the censer and then stood up and nodded. "I'll do my best. The black market is tricky, but I have a few contacts that will give me a good place to start."

"I'd like to keep my name out of it if you can," Daphne said.

"Of course. I saw you on the morning news a week or so ago, so I'll use that to explain my interest," Lee said. "I'll find where this came from."

"Don't overpromise," Van said softly.

"I'm not," Lee said with a cheeky grin before she walked to her workstation. As soon as she sat down, her fingers started flying over one of the keyboards.

Kenji turned back to Van. "Can you keep this in the safe overnight?"

"Of course."

"I want to turn it over to the police tomorrow but would like to keep it quiet," Daphne said. "I don't know many detectives. Is there anyone you trust who can help with that?"

"I know a detective. I'll reach out to her and set something up," Van said. "Will you be here all day tomorrow?"

Kenji shook his head. "We're going to the museum in the morning, and then we can be back—"

"I have other clients, Kenji. I'll have to go by my office and work," Daphne interrupted him.

"Not a problem. I'll have her come after hours," Van

said. "The security team is at your house now, and I'll let you know when they are done."

"Great." There was a pause as she glanced around the room. "Will I be able to go back home soon?" Daphne asked.

"That's up to Kenji," Van said.

Daphne turned to look at him, and he just shrugged. "We'll see how tomorrow goes."

He led her out of the computer room after she watched Van put the censer in the safe with hawk eyes. He allowed her to change the key code, and both Kenji and Van looked away as she set the new code and closed the door. Now she was the only one who could get to the item.

He heard her walking quietly behind him with her wheeled suitcase down the corridor to the elevator. They got off on the floor that was split by a short hallway between his very roomy apartment and Xander's.

Someone had put a Master Chief figure from *Halo* inside the wreath on his door, with a small Santa hat glued onto his helmet. Kenji laughed when he saw it, knowing full well it had to be Xander, who made *Warhammer* figures in his downtime.

"That's…one of a kind," Daphne said.

"Yeah. I'm not much on Christmas, but the team tries to get me into it," he said.

"Who's that?" she asked, pointing to the figure.

"Master Chief from *Halo*. He's the guy that you play as in the game," he said. He really didn't want to talk about gaming, Daphne always seemed too refined for it, but at least it was giving him another moment before he took her into his place.

"Did you play that when we were together?" she asked. "I know you did some shooting games."

"Yeah. It came out in 2001. It's a massive multiplayer game, so I would play it online sometimes."

"Did I ever play it?"

"Maybe. It's set in space, and we fight aliens," he said.

She just shook her head as she removed her ponytail holder, causing her hair to fall over her shoulder. He reached out and pushed it back behind her ear. He should have been keeping his hands off her, but it was hard.

That one kiss had opened memories he'd shoved deep down and away for a good reason. This was no time to be turned on by her. Her place had been broken into. She had a stolen museum item. Not to mention the fact that he'd been hired to be her bodyguard because she'd been shot at and likely remained at risk.

But he still wanted her. More than he'd expected.

There was no way around that. Standing in front of his home. The one place that he was most himself. And he was about to bring her into it. He felt vulnerable in a way that he seldom admitted.

But with Daphne, he was totally willing to lose his armor, and it was freaking him out. He would stand out here all day talking about *Halo* if it meant he didn't have to take her inside, where there was the biggest chance he'd break the oath he made to himself when he'd first accepted that she was his client.

He wasn't going to sleep with her.

Period.

Not that his body gave a crap about promises. Everything masculine in him was on point and ready to pull her into his arms and see just how much they had changed in the years they'd been apart.

But that wasn't the man he was. Not today, and not when he was working. He knew that. It was just…

"My place isn't much."

She put her hand on his forearm, and he looked down at her long manicured fingers where she touched him. A slow, steady beat had started inside of him.

"I'm sure it's cleaner and safer than mine."

Kenji took a deep breath before he used his key fob to open the door. He'd never blurred the lines between personal and professional before, but from the moment Daphne's name had come up, he'd known there was no way around it this time.

Chapter 7

The apartment was one big open room with en suite bedrooms off to either side. The kitchen was chef-grade and had a large island with two stools at it. Meanwhile, the living room had a huge TV—she'd never seen one that large before—with a console underneath it. There were bookshelves all along one of the walls, floor-to-ceiling and stuffed with books of all kinds. There was a couch in front of the TV and two large leather recliners on either side.

She moved into the room, towing her suitcase behind her. Kenji dropped his keys in a bowl on the table in the entryway and then toed off his shoes. She bent to unzip the boots she was wearing before taking them off.

"Nice place," she said, faintly echoing what he'd said when they'd pulled up to her house.

"I don't know my dad, so I have no idea what he thinks of it," Kenji said with a wry grin. "Your bedroom is on the right. There's a nice-size bath in there if you were serious about wanting one."

"Thanks, I was," she said.

"I'm going to have Xander come and hang in the living room while I shower," he said.

"I thought I was safe here."

"You are, but I don't like to take chances," he said. "I should have checked the alleyway at the coffee shop."

"There was no one out there. The only threat was from me being reckless," she said, walking over to him and putting her hand on his shoulder. "I'm not holding that against you."

"I am," he said.

Kenji held himself to a higher standard than anyone else she knew. That was saying a lot given the demands she put on herself to be the best. She suspected, though they'd never had a chance to talk at length about their parents, that it had something to do with the father he'd never met.

He'd told her that one late night when they'd been studying together. For the life of her, she couldn't understand how someone would just walk away from their own child. She knew everyone followed their own path and had their own reasons. It was really…seeing Kenji and the effect that absent man had on him made her furious. Even without being in his son's life, he'd influenced Kenji's.

"Okay about your friend," she said.

"I wasn't asking permission," he said sardonically.

"I'm the client, right? Doesn't that make me the boss?"

"You are the client, but you are definitely not the boss," he said.

A spark of mischief and excitement went through her. For the first time that evening, she didn't feel tired or scared. Even her shoulder was simply a dull ache and not in real pain. And Kenji was acting like *Kenji* and not like an ultra-efficient bodyguard. That meant more to her than she wanted it to.

"Is that a Daphne rule or every client rule?" she teased.

"Every client, but especially you."

"Why?"

"Clients are reckless, and don't think they can be killed. They take risks that put them in danger, and that's why the bodyguard is always in charge."

"I can't be killed with you watching over me, Kenji. That is one thing I know for certain. And I bet your other clients do as well," she said, then leaned up and kissed him quickly on the lips because she wanted to. Then winked and pivoted away, towing her suitcase toward the room he'd indicated would be hers.

Busy congratulating herself on throwing him off his guard, she completely missed him coming up behind her. He turned her around and pulled her into his arms, being careful of her injured shoulder, and brought his mouth down on hers.

She stopped thinking and almost stopped breathing as her instincts took over. This was what she needed. This moment to feel safe and like a woman, not an international attorney who was working on a case that had turned very dangerous. Just Daphne.

Kenji was probably the one person in the world that she truly had ever let her guard down with. Her parents had always had a high standard that Daphne had never felt like she lived up to.

But until he left, Kenji had made her feel like she was enough.

Shutting down her mind, she put her hands in his hair. It was thick and silky and felt good under her fingers. She angled her head to the side as his tongue slid deeper into her mouth. His hands moved down her back, cupping her butt as he lifted her more fully into contact with his body. She put one hand on his hip, drawing herself closer, lifting one leg over his thigh so that the ridge of his cock rubbed against her center.

He squeezed her butt cheek, and she moaned. As he thrust his hips forward, she shivered with need. She pulled her head back, their eyes met, and she wanted nothing more than to take him to bed and pretend for a brief moment that her life wasn't the mess it had become.

He brushed his thumb over her lower lip, looking as if he were going to say something, when there was a knock on the door.

He stepped back, steadying her as he did so. "That'll be Xander."

"Okay then," she said, continuing to make her way into the bedroom.

As soon as she was there, she closed the door and leaned back against it. She heard the rumble of another voice talking to Kenji but stood there rather than opening the door. It was too soon to show herself to someone else. Her pulse was racing, her body was on fire, and all she could think about was how glad she was that Kenji was here with her.

She might not know the reason why he'd left her, but he was here now. After the night she'd just had, that suited her. If her life was in danger and her current case wasn't turning into a big puzzle, she might feel differently, but it was. These heart-pounding feelings would just have to wait.

* * *

Xander was his best friend, probably the one person he felt most comfortable with. But right now, he could have done without the intrusion, or at least that's how his body felt. His mind was glad X once again had his back. Whether his friend knew it or not.

"Thanks for coming over. We've had a rough night. I need a shower, and I… I just don't trust her to stay put."

Kenji was glad that Daphne hadn't intuited that was the reason he'd asked Xander to cover for him.

"Why not?"

"She's independent and used to doing her own thing. Plus this case means a lot to her," Kenji said. "Which is fine. We can talk more about it, but after I've showered."

"No problem. I've got your back."

"Thanks, man."

Kenji left his friend in the living area and went into his own bedroom. As soon as he closed the door, all of the emotions he'd repressed since the beginning of the day flooded out. He walked to the punching bag in the corner and dropped into a fighting stance, kicking and punching it until he was sweating. Then he shook his head, exhausted but still tense, and went to the shower.

Daphne wasn't what he'd expected. *Duh.* How could a woman who he'd just seen in pictures for almost twelve years be real. She was an amalgam of the girl he'd known and what he'd seen of her that one time he'd almost talked to her after the CIA.

She was smart, flirty, fierce and sassy, all things he remembered. But age had honed those things and made her into a woman who was damned hard for him to resist. He wasn't sure he could trust her to do anything but find evidence to win her case. She wasn't going to put herself first, and he wasn't going to be able to convince her to do otherwise.

Which, as he soaped his body, shouldn't have been as exciting a thought as it was. Yes, it would be difficult, but protecting Daphne was the first case he'd had since he'd left the CIA that made him feel this alive.

Part of it was the sexual attraction. He wasn't going to front and act like that didn't matter. If X hadn't knocked when he had, Kenji would have had her up against the wall next to her bedroom, and he was damned sure that Daphne would have enjoyed it.

But that wasn't why she was here. He had to keep reminding himself. He was supposed to keep her safe, not act out his wild fantasies with her.

So that meant shadowing her every move, having Lee run down where the censer had come from, and keeping his dick in his pants and his hands to himself.

No matter that she'd kissed him first. He had to have better control over himself, and he usually did. For her, he had to be the best version of the bodyguard he always was. Not a man too caught up in his hormones to do his job.

He finished his shower, blow-dried his hair, and then got dressed in some black sweatpants and a matching tee. When he came into the living room, Xander had the Xbox on and was playing *Halo*.

Kenji grabbed a couple of nutritious energy drinks from the fridge and then vaulted over the back of the couch and picked up a controller to join the game.

"Any movement from her room?"

"Nothing. I'll leave after this match," Xander said.

"Obie's got an exam this week, so I'm staying a few extra days. Need me for anything?"

Kenji caught Xander up on the case and the fact that they were trying to figure out if there was a black market art dealer involved. "If Lee finds someone, maybe you could help locate them."

"Yeah. No problem," he said.

They continued playing *Halo* until they won the co-op team match they were on. Xander finished his energy drink and then stood up. "You good?"

"Yeah. See you tomorrow."

Xander left the apartment and Kenji settled in on the couch, knowing that he'd probably stay here all night. He'd get some rest in the leather recliner, but he wanted to keep an eye on Daphne's door.

Meanwhile he played another co-op match, and Xander popped up on the opposite team. He had fun hunting down his friend and killing him in the game since the stakes in their real life were higher and more serious. As the match ended, Daphne's door opened, and she came out into the room.

"Oh, I thought you'd be in bed," she said.

He exited the game, putting down his controller. "Nope. You thinking of running?"

"Not at all. Having my house broken into scared me enough to stay put for now," she said. "I couldn't sleep. I have insomnia, and my sleep therapist advises against doing anything other than sleeping in bed. I thought I'd come and find a book to read."

She wore a pair of red silk pajamas and had bare feet as she moved through the living room toward the bookshelves.

She read a few of the spines while he watched her, and then stopped and turned. "We never got to finish our personal conversation."

"And you want to now?"

She shrugged and pushed her hair behind her ear. "Maybe. I can't help thinking about what happened between us today and in college. I want to separate the two, but it's not that easy. After you, I never really trusted my feelings again."

That was hard to hear, but it was her right to say this to him. "I never meant for that to happen."

"I know, so why'd you leave like that?" she asked. Her voice was strong and didn't waver. She just looked at him, right into his soul, and he knew she deserved the truth no matter how difficult telling it would be for him.

He exhaled long and hard and then rubbed his hand against the back of his neck. "Sit down and I'll tell you."

Sitting curled up in the leather recliner in Kenji's apartment felt like she'd stepped out of her life and into an alternate reality. He hadn't really changed in the years since they'd been together. The kisses they'd shared reminded her that, even now, she still wanted him. Wouldn't it be nice if physical attraction equaled shared feelings on both sides?

Life didn't work that way, something she'd known for a while. There was still a part of her that was desperately trying to figure out why Kenji was the man she could never forget. Why was he the one man she wanted, no matter that he'd hurt her before and he wasn't really in her life?

He made her feel safe. But surely her gut could be…
What was her gut even saying?

Kenji had asked her to sit down and then he'd tell her
the truth, but he was still struggling to find the words.

He offered her a drink. Asked her if she wanted a
blanket. She shook her head to both.

"Just tell me. Was it that you never cared?" she asked.
"I think the part I struggle the most with is the fact that
I loved you the way I did, and you didn't."

Her dad always said that after midnight, the truth
had a way of coming out. He was right. She'd gotten
the truth from witnesses and clients after the witching
hour, which was great. But her dropping truth bombs on
Kenji wasn't exactly what she wanted. It cut them both
too deeply. Where was her sense of self-preservation?

Did she really need this lethally sexy bodyguard from
her past to affirm that he'd never really cared?

"No, Daph. It was never that. I cared too much," he
said.

"Sure."

He shoved his hand through that fall of bangs, and
of course it artfully fell right back into place. But she'd
rattled him. Which surprised and intrigued her.

"I had an idea of who I was, the kind of man I would
be and how I would live my life. That plan didn't include
a dark-haired woman who distracted me from that path
and showed me an alternative life."

"Distracted you?"

"Yes. You must know I was obsessed with you and
the life you gave me a glimpse of. I watched you sleep
in my arms, and glimpses of a family and future together teased the edges of my mind," he said. Leaning

forward, he put his elbows on his thighs and steepled his fingers together as he stared at the carpet.

She had dreams of a future, too. Why had he left? She'd heard what he said about a different path but still couldn't understand the break he'd made between the two of them. "Why didn't you just say you weren't ready for us?"

"There was no way to walk both paths."

There was a finality to his words that made her heart ache a little bit. "Of course there was. You just didn't see it."

"Perhaps. We were young, and I still had a lot to prove to myself and to the CIA. I wanted the excitement and danger they were promising," he said.

"I know that part," she admitted. He'd been clear about anticipating the missions he'd be sent on with gusto. Kenji and she both had wanted to make the world a better place. He had done it by going on covert missions and doing things that she probably would never know about. She'd done it in the courts, seeking justice a different way, and she was happy with her choice.

Was Kenji?

"Yeah, you do. I never meant to hurt you. I figured…"

"What, that I didn't really love you, so when I begged you not to go and cried my eyes out, you thought I'd be fine the next day?" she asked. For the love of all that was holy, why was her mind not censoring her thoughts?

"No. God, no. I just figured you'd write me off as not worthy."

There it was, she thought. The truth that had been buried in all of Kenji's other explanations. Not being worthy was a big part of who he was. "You were always worthy. I know your mom would have wanted you to know that too. *He* wasn't worthy. It was never about you."

"But it was always about him," Kenji said. "I've been to a therapist in the last few years, so I know what you're saying is right. In my head, it makes perfect sense. Fuck that dude who didn't want to know his son, right?"

"In your heart, it's not that easy."

Logic and emotions worked that way. No matter how many times she told herself it didn't matter that she'd never been close to her mom, that she was lucky to have her relationship with her father, Daphne still longed for that bond. She missed it in a way that had left an emptiness inside of her.

She saw the same emptiness in Kenji. Part of her wondered if that had been what had drawn them together. That need to prove something and to fill that chasm in their hearts and souls with saving the world.

That was something she doubted she'd ever find the answer to.

"No, it's not. But the man I am today wouldn't make that choice, Daphne. If you hear nothing else from me tonight, hear this. I walked away because I knew if I didn't, I'd choose you, and I was afraid I'd end up resenting that choice."

His words didn't fix the past, but she had a better understanding for why he'd left her the way he had. Why he'd felt that the only solution was a clean break. And maybe why she was finding it so hard to resist him now that he was back in her life.

It wasn't just that he had made her feel safe. It wasn't just that he was strong and still so sexy she ached to have him inside of her when they were in the same room. It was that she saw the same lost soul she'd once connected with, and she wanted to connect with him again.

Chapter 8

Raw emotion and the past were two things he'd never been keen to spend much time dwelling on. Right now his skin felt too tight, but inside his stomach, that knot he'd had since she'd first asked him why he'd left her started to loosen. Confession was good for the soul.

Van touted that often, and for the first time, Kenji almost got what his boss had been talking about. Maybe if he'd been honest with her back in the day…but he knew he couldn't have been. He had needed to go on the journey he'd been on to get to the man he was today.

"I needed to hear that," she said. "Thank you."

He nodded, keeping that stoic look on his face even though inside he was a seething storm that was ready for a downpour. He knew that he needed to just ride this out. Let her set the boundaries and he'd respect them.

There was something so mature about the way Daphne handled herself, and he struggled to meet it. He knew part of the reason was that he'd never really trusted anyone. His mom had been his one stalwart during his childhood, and having her die as soon as he went to college had shaken him to his core.

Moving into the Price Tower had forced him to drop

his guard slightly over time, becoming friends with the team. That had been easier because they were all loners who'd been hiding something. Time had made them all relax, and true bonds had been forged between them.

But this was Daphne. The woman he'd known when he'd been that lost boy before he'd become the man he was today. It was harder with her because in his gut, he still wanted to impress her.

He was on a case with probably the one client he most wanted to keep safe. Daphne acting measured and polite was the best outcome he could hope for. So why did it make him want to punch something or maybe go to the shooting range on the third floor and fire his weapon at a target until it passed?

"I know that I should say something, but I have no idea what would help either of us," she said. "Work is what I fall back on when life is like this."

"Of course." Her words made sense. Like his own path, the path she'd chosen was dominated by her job. "Want to strategize for tomorrow when we go to the museum?"

"Yeah, I'd love that. Let me get my notepad. I think better on paper," she said.

He watched her get up and walk back to her room. Her hips swayed with each step she took, and he couldn't tear his eyes from her. His gut ached for something that he could have had. Regret wasn't his deal. But remorse, yeah, he had that.

It had been his decision. He'd chosen to leave something that he was pretty sure he wanted again more than anything and wasn't sure that he would ever have.

She turned and noticed him staring at her. "Kenji?"

Busted. "Nothing. I'll get my tablet. I think better on devices," he said, forcing himself to smile and wink at her.

Which made her raise both eyebrows as she tipped her head to the side. "Is it okay for us to be friendly?"

Yeah, because when was he ever a smiling and winking guy? *Never.*

"Okay how?"

"I mean with you as my bodyguard. In that Whitney Houston movie, it didn't end well for them."

"We're not in a movie, and I think it's going to be hard for us not to be friendly given our past. As long as I don't lose objectivity, we should be good."

"How would that happen?" she asked.

"Depends on you, I guess," he said.

She licked her lips, and he wanted to groan as his eyes tracked the movement. He was definitely biased, but she had the best damned mouth he'd ever seen. Because he'd kissed her, he knew that it was still as soft and welcoming as it had been back in the day.

God, he wanted to kiss her again.

"I'll get my tablet."

He stood and walked to his desk in the corner of the living room and grabbed his tablet. The personal stuff was over. He was going to be the consummate bodyguard when she came back in.

He wouldn't allow his mind to drift to her body and all the ways he'd like to touch her. He wouldn't look at her mouth when she spoke and remember how it felt when he'd kissed her last, hot and addictive. He wouldn't allow his hormones to come into play, even though his blood felt hotter and heavier and his erection stirred when she returned to the living room and sat down on the couch next to him.

She smelled of peaches and cream, and her smile was soft and gentle. Did she know that she was driving him out of his mind? Would it matter if she did? Too much had passed between them for there to be any hope of a new relationship now.

"You used to be a really good judge of people. Are you still?" she asked.

"Usually. Want me to observe?"

"Yes. I'm meant to meet Lauder again and someone from the archives. I imagine there might be a few other museum staff that we will come into contact with," she said.

"Should I photograph them?" The camera often showed things that the naked eye didn't catch.

"No. I think putting my staff on edge is one thing, but this is different. What I want is for you to just observe them and maybe make notes on each person. I need to verify if the items are getting out of the museum some-how, and either Lauder or someone on his staff knows something about it."

He agreed. "Tell me more about the items. Do you have a catalog of them?"

"I have a list with descriptions and item numbers from the museum. The exhibit they held in 1985 when they first received the items was covered by several local newspapers and magazines. But these are the only pho-tos I have."

She air-dropped him some scanned images from her phone along with the inventory PDF. He opened them, scanning the list, and eventually landed on the censer she had found in the alleyway. "How many items besides the censer are missing?"

"Fourteen," she said. Then she took a paper from the folio that had her notepad in it. "But over the last five years, seventeen different items have been marked missing and then returned to the collection. I have subpoenaed the museum's financial records, but the judge hasn't ruled if I can see them and if they are relevant to the case."

"Why do you think they are?"

"I want to see if there is an influx or outflux of cash around the time the items were returned. I have two theories."

"And they are?" He liked watching her mind work, and he imagined this was how she got ready for her court cases. Outlining all the possible ways something could go and then preparing for them.

"One: someone in the museum is selling them, and then the museum is buying them back to hide or cover for the theft and sale." She wriggled her eyebrows at him as she said that.

"Possibly," he said. Waiting to hear her other theory before weighing in on it. He was always better when he could see the entire picture. He'd been working with her for a short while, but already he was starting to form an idea of what was going on here.

Could there be two players instead of one, as Daphne was postulating? It seemed obvious that the attacks on Daphne were tied to her case. But she'd said that the shooter had waited at the end of the alleyway and watched her until she called 911. The cops would have searched the area, but the shooter could have left after they arrived.

Were the attacks on Daphne personal and not related to her case? He wasn't going to mention that to her. Not yet. He needed to hear more of her theory.

"Yeah, I know there are a lot of holes in that one. I mean, why wouldn't the museum just fire the person who is selling them? My second theory is that the museum needs money and is selling the pieces to fund an exhibit or operating costs and then rebuying them. Sort of like putting them in a pawn shop. Which I guess is kind of like theory number one, but instead of personal gain, it's to keep the museum afloat."

Money was a strong motivator, and the way the items were simply missing instead of stolen was interesting. Also, some had been missing and then "found" later. "Do you think the judge will grant your request?"

"I have no idea. She was completely right when she said that money isn't what my case is about. The case is supposed to be about finding out who the items belong to and restoring them to their rightful owner. Money shouldn't be a player in this."

"But it usually is," he said.

"Exactly."

Talking with Kenji eased a lot of the tension in her mind. He asked insightful questions and offered avenues that she hadn't considered. The distraction from the day was helpful, but she still wasn't sure she could sleep. Plus a part of her didn't want to leave Kenji.

He probably needed some rest before tomorrow. If he'd been a stranger, more than likely she wouldn't have been hanging out in the living room with him, trying to find reasons to stay awake. Which was really all the answer she needed. "Am I keeping you up?"

He shook his head as he put his tablet on the coffee table. "No. I was planning to stay out here all night."

Something wasn't adding up. He'd brought her here because her place had been burgled. But was there something about the tower she didn't know? "Why? Aren't we safe here?"

"You totally are," he said, stretching his arm out along the back of the couch. "I just don't like surprises, like the one I got tonight when you slipped away from me."

She blushed when he said it. In retrospect, it had been extremely stupid of her to do that. But she was tired of all the back-and-forth in this case and waiting for a break. Sometimes she knew she had to make one for herself. "Sorry for sneaking out on you. I just wasn't sure you'd be down for going back out there."

He pulled his arm down and leaned toward her. There was so much intensity in his face and the way he held his body.

"I am down for keeping you safe, we clear?" he said, but it was clearly an order, not a question.

She wrinkled her nose at him. "If you didn't phrase that way, then yes."

"When it comes to your safety—"

She cut him off. "I know, you are in charge. But do you have to sound like a bossy douchebag?"

"That's usually the only effective way to make sure a client listens to me. There isn't room to debate when your life is on the line."

She'd forgotten that he wasn't here for her personally.

This was professional. Kenji was a bodyguard and used to putting himself in the line of fire to keep his clients safe. Of course there wasn't room for debate.

"Fair enough. I don't actually think my life is on the line."

Or rather, she didn't want to believe that. The shooter had hit her in the shoulder, and her house had been burgled while she wasn't there. That had to mean they wanted the object and were willing to hurt her, but not kill her. *Right?*

"Maybe, maybe not. But I'm not taking any chances. The fact that both these incidents have happened so close together makes me believe that they will escalate. Unless you want to put the censer back in the alleyway."

"No. It needs to be in police custody so I can track what happens to it," she said.

He held his hands up, and she realized she'd been a bit forceful. "Guess you're not the only bossy douchebag in the room."

"Nice to know I have company," he said with a wry smile.

His smile made her heartbeat speed up, and there she was, thinking of him again. Not as her bodyguard or the man from her past who had her hurt her. But the guy she'd fallen for...the guy she still missed. "Will we be staying here from now on?"

"I guess it depends on what you stir up tomorrow. If I think you will be safe at your home, we can stay there."

"You'll stay with me?" she asked him. The thought of being alone right now was frightening, which she knew was logical given the last few days. But she'd always been a strong woman and had no problem living on her own.

She'd been afraid to have a roommate in case…well, in case there was something about her that was off-putting. Kenji had left her, and before that, her mom had loathed her. Was there something unfavorable about living with her that she was unaware of?

She hadn't wanted to risk it, so she had simply always lived on her own. Now she was afraid to be alone. God, this was a mess. It would have been nice if she had some easy solution that she could just pull out and get the case before the judge and win.

"Until the threat to you is gone," he said.

"So after my case," she said.

"If you're safe," he returned.

"Why wouldn't I be?"

"I don't know yet. But I'm just keeping all avenues open."

"Like what else?"

"That someone doesn't want you around, and it has nothing to do with the case."

"But the missing items…"

"Are missing. You'll figure out if there is a crime there," he said. "I'm going to figure out who's threatening you and neutralize the threat."

That made her feel safe all the way to her core. She knew Carl didn't like it when his attorneys were put in the line of fire. And this case shouldn't have been one to do so. Hiring Price, hiring Kenji, had been the right decision.

"What about Christmas?" she asked.

"What about it?"

"My case will go into January. Will you take the holiday off?"

"If the threat to you has passed," he reiterated.

Would it? Christmas was an odd time of year for her. She liked it, sort of. The way everyone was happier in the office was pleasant. Her dad always sent her a nice gift and some years came out to visit her. But then there was the other side. Remembering the years when her mom had still been alive. They weren't the best memories or the happiest Christmases.

"You okay?" he asked.

"Yeah," she said. She wasn't about to share that part of her life with him. She'd grown up in a very privileged home and had wanted for nothing material. She'd had the nicest clothes, gone to the best schools and been given many advantages. Talking about the fact that her mom hadn't loved her and had resented her wasn't something she was going to bring up.

She dealt with it internally as she always had.

"Christmas isn't really something I celebrate since my mom died," Kenji said. "But if you have traditions or things you want to do, we can do them here. Van always orders trees for all of us."

"All of you?" she asked, seizing on Kenji's holiday spirit instead of her own.

"The entire team has living quarters here. Mostly because our assignments take us out of town for long stretches of time."

"Interesting. How many are there?"

"Just six of us. Well, five now that Luna is living with her husband at his penthouse, but it's not too far from here," he said.

"Xander lives across the hall from you. Where does everyone else live?" she asked.

"Rick and Luna used to share the floor above us. Lee has an apartment on the same level as her computer room, and Van has the top floor to himself. I don't usually decorate the tree or anything, but we could if you wanted to."

Did she want to try to make this Christmas different?

Of course she did. She'd bought some ornaments the year that Kenji had dumped her but had never put them up. This year, with Cass, she had finally started to feel like she had some traditions. Maybe it was time to stop dwelling in that space where she wasn't worthy of the love and joy of the holiday season.

"I'd like that."

"I think I would too," he said. "You should head to bed. I imagine you're an up-early person."

"You know I am."

"I wasn't sure if that had changed," he said.

"It hasn't. I guess you're still a night owl." He'd always been awake long after she drifted off to sleep. He'd come into their bed late at night, make love to her and then crash, which had always felt special and sexy to her

"I am. But the job has made me alert all the time," he said. "Thanks for listening tonight."

"Thanks for opening up. I needed to hear it," she said, gathering her stuff. Then she got up and went into the bedroom he'd assigned her.

Closing the door behind her, she looked at the bed and wished she had the courage to ask him to sleep with her. But she wasn't ready for that. Not tonight. She had too much on her mind. The case, the person or people who'd been in her house, the past with her mom and how she'd felt if she could be perfect, maybe she'd be lovable. And the past with Kenji, when she'd learned that even her version of perfection wasn't enough...

Until tonight, when he'd told her that who she was *had* been enough.

Chapter 9

Dressed and ready for the day, Daphne realized her shoulder was starting to hurt a little bit less, and she'd even managed a few hours of sleep after leaving Kenji. He was dressed in another slim-fitting black suit and tie with a white shirt. He even had on dark sunglasses to combat the sun in LA. Growing up on the East Coast, December had been cold and gray with snow or rain. It hadn't taken her long to adjust to the sunny climate in LA. Though it did get cold, most days even in December saw sun.

She had her sunglasses on as well feeling like they were agents in a thriller. She watched Kenji has he drove. His hands on the wheel were strong, and she had never felt safer in a vehicle, even though he was going a little over the speed limit. The traffic wasn't too heavy since they'd left after rush hour. When he pulled into the parking lot of the Los Angeles Museum of Foreign Cultures, she realized she'd spent most of the drive thinking about him instead of reviewing her day.

Blaming it on the lack of sleep was one thing, but she couldn't let that happen again.

The Los Angeles Museum of Foreign Cultures was

on the stretch of Wilshire Boulevard that extended between Fairfax Avenue and La Brea Avenue, home to the famous tar pits. Her offices were on Wilshire, so it wasn't that far of a drive to get to it. The Los Angeles parks department had been busy putting up the holiday lights for the season, and as they drove by them, she couldn't help but wonder about Kenji and Christmas. It was only a few weeks away, and his apartment didn't show any signs of it. She was tempted to ask him about it, maybe take him up on his offer to decorate, but not today when she had to stay focused on getting answers.

The museum was situated on the end of Museum Row. It was one of the smaller establishments but well-known for its rare antiquities. That was part of the reason that Pierce was so determined to hold on to the collection.

The Maqdala collection that had been donated by Hazelton-Measham was unusual in North America, with the only other items housed in Canada at the Royal Ontario Museum. It gave the Los Angeles Museum of Foreign Cultures some cachet in that regard. Many of the collections at this museum were rare and popular. In the museum world, a collection that was both unique and commercially viable was invaluable.

The museum's building was in itself an architectural masterpiece created by the architect I.M. Pei. Like many of Pei's designs, this one had a modern sensibility that made the most of the outdoor space around it. It felt like it was part of the landscape while standing out and drawing the eye. She'd always liked the building. Daphne understood why the museum was fighting so hard to keep the collection. She understood that this loss might bring more lawsuits to them, but that was something many museums were facing in this day and age.

The parking lot was large and usually full, and there was a banner across the front advertising a *Night at the Museum*–style event for the upcoming Christmas season. Two more banners invited visitors to check out winter traditions from around the world. Leading up to the entrance, there was a reflecting pond in the middle of two long lawns that snaked up to a set of wide concrete stairs. There was a large art installation that spelled out Happy Holidays positioned along one of them, facing the parking lot entrance.

The letters showed celebrations from around the world and used the iconography associated with them, which Daphne had first learned when she'd gone on the news to discuss her case. She knew that many were divided on her case, but the only person who needed to hear her was the judge. Thankfully, Judge Mallon wasn't one to be swayed by public sentiment. The case would be judged on facts and merit.

The most salient fact was that Hazelton-Measham, as a soldier in the British expedition, hadn't been granted the right by anyone to loot the church and the treasury and bring the items home with him. Having donated them to the museum…well, Daphne believed they should be returned to Amba Mariam. She hoped that the judge would see this evidence as critically as she did.

Pulling herself out of her legal haze, she reached for the handle of the front door of the car, but Kenji hit the locks.

She glanced over at him.

"I will get out first and then come around so I'm in position," he said. "Are you taking a bag in with you?"

"Yes. I take this thing everywhere," she said, gesturing to her big Louis Vuitton shoulder bag.

"This parking lot is exposed, and there is no way for me to know if there are shooters—

"Kenji, I'm not worried here. I don't think whoever is behind this is going to attack me here."

"I'm not taking any chances. Keep your bag close, and if I tell you to run, go to the left corner of the entrance that's protected on two sides. Get small behind the trash can," he ordered.

"Okay," she said. His seriousness was making her more aware of her surroundings, and the remaining sleepiness that had been around her like a heavy pashmina dissipated. Kenji got out of the car in one swift motion, and she noticed he'd unbuttoned his jacket. When he moved, his hand was on the holster at his hip.

It made her very aware of the dangerousness of the situation she found herself in. It had been hard to believe the threat to her life was real when she was with Kenji, but now this visit didn't seem like just another morning errand she had to run.

He opened her door and she stepped out, quickly moving to close the door behind her. Kenji put hand at the small of her back and urged her to scurry quickly across the parking lot. Another car pulled in just as they reached the museum entrance. He immediately put his body between her and the vehicle, moving her into the corner that he'd mentioned she should use. The car pulled into a spot, and no one appeared to get out.

"Can we go inside?" she asked.

"Yes, stay in front of me. When we move inside, don't stop until you are at the desk."

She just nodded. The tension in Kenji was palpable. This glimpse of the professional that he'd become was showing her another side to him. As much as she might have wished last night that he'd stayed with her all those years ago, he wouldn't have become this man. And the world needed men like Kenji in it.

People who were willing to put their lives on the line to protect others.

She continued with him as he directed them into the museum. They walked to the reception desk, which was manned by a uniformed security guard and an older woman who smiled as they entered.

The security guard nodded at Kenji as they entered the building. The other man held himself the way Xander did, shoulders back and standing at attention. So Kenji clocked him as ex-military. He wanted to let the security guard know he was carrying his weapon. He also hoped to get some extra information from the man. "Hi there. I'm Kenji Wada with Price Security and the bodyguard for Ms. Amana." Kenji held out his hand.

"Paul Richards. Head of security here at the museum. Pierce let us know about Ms. Amana's attack."

"What did he say?"

"Just that she'd been shot at and that we should be on alert when she came here. Like I'm not always watching everyone who comes in and out of the museum."

Kenji heard the irritation in the other man's voice. He also found it interesting that Lauder had mentioned the incident. "I'm carrying and licensed for concealed.

Other than the cameras and alarms on the pieces, do you have other passive security measures?"

"Yeah. Why?"

"Ms. Amana is trying to find some pieces labeled as missing, and your boss insists they haven't been stolen. I was wondering if there was any security footage to look at," Kenji said, glancing over at Daphne. It was her case, and he was aware that he was probably overstepping, but if he could help her out, he wanted to.

"We do have security footage, but I can't just hand it over," Paul said, rubbing the back of his neck and then running his hand over the top of his head. Almost as if he were nervous.

"Don't worry. I wasn't asking to see it. Ms. Amana will go through the courts to get a look at it," Kenji said before nodding at the guard and heading back over to Daphne.

The receptionist, Laverne, recognized Daphne and greeted her by name. "I'm sorry to say that Mr. Lauder is out sick today. He asked that one of the archivists, Grey Joy, show you around and assist you in your search. I'll let her know you are here."

Laverne had curly red hair that framed her full face. She had on sparkly gold eyeshadow and thick eyelashes that had to be fake. They fell to her cheeks whenever she blinked. She wore a puffy-sleeved top that fell to a deep vee neckline, and when she crossed her arms and leaned forward, the medallion necklace she wore swung forward.

She kept chatting away, and Daphne knew she should be paying attention to what the other woman was saying, but her eyes had caught a note on Laverne's desk. It read *C. 4 pm.* Seemed oddly cryptic for a receptionist's note.

There was also a pamphlet for the museum's Arts of Africa exhibit, which currently had a banner over it that said Temporarily Closed. That was her doing, Daphne thought. She'd filed to have the museum stop profiting off showing the contested goods until the matter was resolved.

Laverne noticed her looking at the pamphlet. "Yeah. That's sort of slowed down foot traffic. We used to get a lot of people who had never seen the Ethiopian Orthodox Church tabots. That collection has really helped to raise awareness here in this area and brought in a lot of researchers who can't get visas to go and visit the sites."

"I'm aware of the cultural significance of it. This case is to return it to the rightful owners, and researchers can always get visas if they follow the proper channels and are honest about what they are in the country for," Daphne pointed out.

Laverne looked like she wanted to argue with Daphne but just smiled at her instead. "I'm sure the courts will figure it all out."

"I am too," Daphne said. She hadn't realized how edgy she was this morning. Maybe it was the lack of sleep, or the fact that someone was after her, but she wasn't herself today.

"Thank you. My bodyguard is with me today, which I believe Mr. Lauder was aware of."

"He was. We were expecting you both," she said. "Would you like any water or coffee while you wait?"

"I'm fine, thank you," she said.

She moved away from the reception desk to the current exhibit behind glass in the foyer. It was a collection of tabots from different churches around the world. She noted that several of them were on loan to the museum, but then she spied that one had been removed for cleaning—and it was one of the items from the Ethiopian Orthodox Church. She had saved the inventory to her phone and quickly found the document and checked the item.

It was on her list, so she'd asked to see it today. She wanted photos of everything that the museum had. There was a chance that more items might go missing, and she wasn't willing to let that happen. This case had been going on for over a year, and because of her caseload—and the museum dragging their feet, in Daphne's opinion—there had been too many delays.

She was ready to wrap this up. Get these objects back in the hands of the people to whom they meant the most.

Kenji came up next to her.

"Lauder is out sick. We're getting a tour by an archivist."

"Name?"

"Grey Joy. Female."

Kenji tapped the earpiece he'd put in that morning before he left. "Lee, museum employees so far are security guard Paul Richards, receptionist Laverne Simpson and archivist Grey Joy."

He then tapped the earpiece again to mute it and turned back to her. "The security guard doesn't know anything about missing pieces and mentioned that the security systems around the museum are top-rate. I've called them and they are sending a rep out to inspect, and my team will find out more."

"Thanks," she said.

Before she could add anything, Grey Joy arrived and led them back to the archives.

Grey had a silver bob that framed her heart-shaped face. Her eyes were wide and large, and she had thick, dark brows. She wore a pair of red-framed glasses and had on a LA Museum of Foreign Cultures collared shirt and a pair of khaki pants. She was shorter than Daphne and wore running shoes that squeaked as they followed her to the back of the archive room.

Daphne looked around as they moved through the large room that was full of floor-to-ceiling shelving units with labeled boxes on them. She wanted to stop and check the boxes, especially when she saw sign on the end of the shelves labeled Ethiopia. She had already asked Pierce if some of the missing items could have been housed incorrectly, which he'd denied.

Maybe Grey would be able to help her in that area. Already Daphne had a list of questions for the other woman. She hoped to get some of the answers about the missing pieces, as well as the piece that she'd found in the alley.

But how was she going to casually bring that up? *So, hey, I found a museum bag behind a coffee shop…any details on how it got there?* Not subtle. Daphne would never be that blunt, because she knew that she had to be careful and have an evidence trail that didn't involve her leading a witness. But she was itching to make her way down the aisle and start opening boxes all the same.

Not that she was going to be able to do that. She paused, taking her phone out of her purse and snapping a photo of the labeling so she could use that in her brief.

They clearly had plenty of other boxes of stored items, and she would like a chance to see what was in them.

"How long have you worked for the museum?" Daphne asked her as they moved into the back rooms. There were floor-to-ceiling metal bookshelves that housed boxes running the length of the room. The floor was corporate tile. There were no windows, which made sense given the items they housed. There were two desks positioned near the front of the room. Both had computer monitors on them and piles of folders as well as coffee mugs.

"For about seven years," Grey said.

Daphne's brow furrowed. "Do you work alone? I notice there are two desks."

"No, there are actually five of us who work down here. But today it's just me, and then Steven will be in later."

"Have we met before?" Daphne asked Grey.

Kenji could tell something was up with the other woman when Grey shook her head vehemently and stepped away from Daphne. "How would we have met?"

"Your voice…you're the one who called me?"

"What? I didn't even know who you were until I was asked to show you around. I think we should focus on that. I've pulled the boxes that we keep the contested items in, and they are on a table back here. Please follow me."

Daphne moved to follow her, but while Grey's back was turned, tapped out a message on her phone and showed it to him.

I think she's the one who I was supposed to meet when I was shot. Should I confront her?

* * *

Kenji wasn't sure what Daphne should do, but this could be the break they were looking for. He scanned the other woman. She was small, so if she was the one who attacked Daphne, he was pretty sure he could subdue her until the authorities arrived.

Daphne raised both eyebrows at him as they reached a table that had several boxes on it. One of them was open. He nodded.

Daphne moved closer to the table, pulling out a burlap bag that matched the one she had found in the alleyway.

"Grey, I believe you are the one who I was meant to meet. You can pretend all you want, but I recognize your voice and this burlap bag."

"I can't talk here."

"Why not? Are you in danger?"

"I just can't—"

Something crashed behind him, and Kenji turned. Seeing something moving out of the corner of his eye, he tackled Daphne to the ground, careful of her injured shoulder and his weight. They lay still as something flew past his head, crashing into the wall behind them, shattering. It looked like one of the mugs that had been on the desks. He put one hand on the floor and shifted to a shooting pose, scanning the area behind them. No one was there, and when he slowly moved to sweep the room, he realized Grey was gone as well.

Daphne was on her feet, running toward the end of the room and the open emergency door. Kenji was right behind in a moment, jogging after her and catching her before she could step through the door.

"No."

"She knows something."

"Someone doesn't want you to talk to her. We'll find her again. We need to secure this room and find out who didn't want you two to talk."

Daphne was pale, and her hands were shaking. "Oh, we are going to get some answers."

"Are you okay?"

"NO! I'm pissed and scared and then pissed that I'm scared. What was that crash, anyway?"

Kenji had her between the wall and his body and looked down into her face, reading the truth of what she was saying. Daphne was a strong woman who could handle herself in any situation, but he felt she was out of patience with this.

"I'm not going to let anything happen to you."

"I know that. But I'd like to get through one day without someone trying to hurt me. I don't believe they were trying to kill me."

"If that mug had connected, you might have gotten a concussion," he said. "But you are right. They seem more intent on injuring you and maybe making you take some time off."

"Well, it's not going to work," she said.

"I believe that," he said, tapping his earpiece. Lee acknowledged him. "We've been attacked in the archives of the museum. Notify the police. I'm going to need everything you can pull on all of the museum employees."

"Are you both okay?"

"We're fine."

"Good. Police on their way. I'll let you know when I have the info you requested."

He tapped his earpiece to mute it. "Cops on their way. I don't want to leave you to go and check the room."

"I have pepper spray."

"Great. I'll wait."

As much as he wanted to find the person who'd attacked Daphne, her safety was his mission. They heard the door that led to the museum open and then footsteps echoing as someone rushed toward them. "Hello?"

"Over here," Kenji said.

"What happened? I'm Dan Jones, the deputy director while Mr. Lauder is out. The emergency door alarm was triggered."

"Someone attacked Daphne and Grey, and Grey ran through the door," Kenji said.

"Who attacked them? I'm so sorry I wasn't here to greet you when you arrived."

"I don't know. I couldn't leave her to go and check. Did you see anyone in the hallway when you came down here?" Kenji asked.

The other man was nervous and kept wringing his hands. "No one. Mr. Lauder is going to be very upset by this. He insisted that your visit go smoothly today, Ms. Amana. Can I get you some tea?"

She shook her head. "No. You can get me all of the items I've requested to see and put them in a secure room for me and my bodyguard to examine. The cops are on their way, and I will be filing a notice with the court that I was attacked while trying to view the evidence in the case."

Dan's eyes went wide, and he used his radio to call for more staff. The room was soon full of people, and Kenji knew he wasn't going to be able to pick up a trail on whomever had attacked them. He wasn't sure that the museum staff were the only ones they should be watching.

"Why weren't you here to greet us?" Kenji asked Dan as they waited.

"Mr. Lauder called in with some last-minute instructions," Dan said.

He wondered if someone had leaked Daphne's schedule. Something he knew she wouldn't take kindly to him bringing up. But he still didn't have all the information on her staff, which was now going to be his top priority.

Chapter 10

Dan was truly the most helpful person in the museum based on her calls and her conversation with Laverne. This was her first time meeting him in person. He wasn't at all what she expected. On the phone, he gave her the impression he was older, taller and bit less nervous than he was right now.

In person, she saw that he was in his late twenties and had thick black hair that curled around his head. He had a thick middle, wore wire-rim glasses, and always seemed easygoing even when she'd talked to him on the phone. So honestly, she was a bit surprised at how young he was.

He wore a suit but no tie and had a lapel pin with the museum's logo on it. He was clearly agitated as he joined them. "Sorry to have kept you waiting."

"That's okay," Daphne said.

"I just spoke to Paul," Kenji said, "and he mentioned you had security footage. I wondered if there was any way that it could be used to see what happened to the missing items."

"Who are you?"

"Kenji Wada, Price Security."

"He's my bodyguard and has been helping out with the different incidents that have been happening to me," Daphne said.

"I'd call being shot at more than an incident," Kenji said.

She just rolled her eyes at him. The last thing she wanted to do was let Dan or anyone else at the museum know she was rattled by all the attacks.

"Paul would know more than me on that. I'm just here to discuss what happened earlier," Dan said. He shoved his hands into his pockets. "I think it would be best if you waited for the police in our offices. Can you follow me?"

Daphne wanted to dig in and keep from leaving the archives. She hadn't really gotten to see anything in the room. Was Grey spooked or had this all been a setup?

Purpose always gave her focus, and she was glad for it as she and Kenji were taken to one of the offices in the museum to await the cops. The office was clearly not used regularly since it only had a pretty standard desk in it, no computer, and only a port for a laptop. The office had one window, which wasn't that large and Kenji immediately moved the desk to the far side of the room away from it.

She was agitated. Not surprising, really, but she'd thought…she'd hoped she would find something in the archives that just neatly pointed to Pierce Lauder as hiding items, and then she'd take that to the courts. Which she knew wasn't realistic, but it would have been nice. Especially after the last few days, she was ready to wrap this case up.

It felt like there was something bigger going on than just these contested items.

She gave her statement to the cops and listened as Kenji gave his. He mentioned to them that she'd been shot four days earlier and that last night someone had broken into her home. Kenji suggested the incidents were all related. The cops took that down before they went to interview the museum staff. Daphne was waiting for the items she'd been meant to view in the archives to be brought to them.

"This attack makes no sense if someone in the museum is involved," Daphne said. "The last thing I would have thought the museum wants is the police here."

"I agree. If the museum or its workers have something to hide, they wouldn't want the cops here. Have you considered that someone might be working on your staff?" he asked.

Daphne closed her eyes and counted to five. She had never had a problem keeping her temper, but she was tired, her shoulder was aching again, no doubt from being dropped to the ground, and her day wasn't going at all to plan. "Stop accusing my staff. I only have people on it who I trust. Why are you so sure it's someone close to me?"

Kenji put his hand up. "I know you trust them, but someone knows where you are going to be before you get there. It makes sense to look at your staff as well as everyone in the museum who you've never met before."

"Don't be sarcastic. It totally doesn't suit you. I know I'm being unreasonable, but honestly, I'm not sure I could handle it if one of my staff is behind this," she said. "I like them. Also, what if I wasn't the target this time? Grey ran as soon as she heard the crash. Maybe the person was after her."

"Possibly."

Kenji said it in a way that made her believe he was trying to pacify her. She knew he was right. At this moment, she couldn't just go around blindly trusting everyone. What was she missing with these items? This case should be straightforward, but when were history and the provenance of taken items ever easy?

The items in this case had been taken by a soldier who had put his life on the line fighting for his country. Maybe they needed to talk to his descendants. She'd received a statement from Henry Hazelton-Measham, but she hadn't talked to him firsthand. "Can I go back to my office?"

"Of course. Once you have finished here, we will go back. I'm going to check in with my team and put your staff's background checks on top priority," he said.

"Great."

The museum staff entered with the boxes, and the acting museum director, Dan Jones, hovered as she carefully examined the items and matched them to her list. None of the missing items were in the boxes, and everything on the inventory matched what she'd been sent.

"I'd go through all of your archives to try to find the missing items."

"I'm not sure—"

"I was just attacked in your museum. I think it might help your case if you make this happen," she said. "Talk to your boss if you need to, and let me know by the end of the day. If I haven't heard back, I'll go through the courts and speak to the press about what happened here today."

Dan stood taller and nodded. "I'll get back with you. Can I see you out now?"

"That would be great. I'd also like to speak to Grey when she returns. Could you ask her to call me?"

"I will," he said, taking Daphne's card.

Kenji moved by her side as they walked through the hallway and out of the museum. The acting director waved them off, and Kenji kept a quick pace as they walked across the parking lot to his car. Once they were inside, he didn't say a word, just put the car in Drive and headed toward her offices.

Putting her mind to sorting through what this latest attack meant kept her composed. Had it even been aimed at her? And like Kenji had suggested, was someone on her team leaking her whereabouts even innocently? Kenji was driving a little faster than usual, and she glanced over at him. He had both hands on the wheel and kept peeking at the review mirror as he wove the car through the traffic.

"Is everything okay?"

"I'm not sure. I think someone is following us," he said.

One of the classes she'd taken when they'd both been at The Farm was in noticing the environment around them and checking for surveillance. It had been years ago, but she did her best to clear her mind of the case and the feeling of insecurity that came from thinking one of staff might not be who they said they were. To dredge up whatever she could remember to help them stay alert.

Kenji drove almost like he was a part of the machine, shifting gears seamlessly as he used the other vehicles around them for cover. "Black Mercedes?" Daphne guessed.

"Yes. Can you read the plate?" he asked.

She couldn't, twisted as she was in her seat. But maybe she'd be able to get a photo of it. She dug her phone out of her bag. Loosening the seat belt, she turned toward the Mercedes.

"Be careful."

"I trust you."

And she totally did. It didn't matter if he annoyed her with his astute observations or that she still wasn't sure about her attraction to him. She knew that he'd die to keep her safe, and there weren't a lot of people she'd say that about. Certainly her mom had never been that dedicated to her. Not sure why that had popped into her head. Except that being around Kenji had always made her feel like she was enough.

Now he wasn't telling her how to take the photo or giving her a lecture on what she should do. He trusted her to get it done. He trusted her—that was the thing that made it easier to be herself. He wasn't looking over at her and trying to see if she was snapping the photo. He knew if it was possible, she'd get one.

She snapped a few, but they were blurry, and finally she got a partial of the plate as Kenji swerved to place them back into the line of traffic from the fast lane. He put his hand in the middle of her back to keep her from flying forward as he hit the brakes to squeeze into the line of cars. There was a blast of horns going off as his maneuver caused others to jack on their brakes.

"Get ready."

Realizing what he was doing, she had the camera on her phone focused as the Mercedes pulled up. Daphne clicked a few times and then hit the photo display to double-check.

"Got it."

As she started to turn, she saw the window on the Mercedes open, a black gloved hand holding a Glock G18 appearing. "He's got a gun."

She doubled her body over to make a small target. Kenji did the same as a bullet hit the driver's-side window. It didn't shatter, and she remembered that he'd told her the car was bulletproof. Lucky break.

The assailant fired again and then stopped as they were in heavier traffic. Daphne looked in her side view mirror. "Shoulder is clear."

Kenji gunned the engine, moving the car off the highway and onto the shoulder. He kept steadily increasing his speed, and she started to turn to check their back tail.

"Don't put yourself in their line of sight. I need you safely in the seat. This is going to be dicey. I can't worry about you," he said.

She put her hands in her lap and sat still and straight. The seat belt was tight and fastened around her body as it should be. Her hands were shaking, so she laced them together. Kenji got to the end of the shoulder as it blended into the exit, cut the car in an impossibly small space, and drove to the shoulder on the opposite side, then continued down the exit ramp and through the red traffic light across several lanes of traffic.

Horns blasted and she heard the squeal of brakes as he got them through the intersection and into the flow of traffic. He continued driving at top speed until they were clear of the area. Then he slowed and started winding through a residential neighborhood. It took a few minutes to realize where they were. He was taking her back to Price Tower.

"We lost them," he said.

"That was some driving," she said. "Thank you."

"You helped by getting the plate," he said. "Thanks for keeping your cool."

She smiled over at him, but he was still watching the road. There was something very sexy about watching Kenji at work. He was so efficient and capable, and he made her feel incredibly safe. Even when he'd been driving fast and making aggressive moves, she'd never once worried he'd allow her to be hurt.

"It reminded me of The Farm a little bit," she said.

"That time we had to try to outmaneuver the instructors. We always made a good team," he said.

They had. "Yeah, we did."

"Why did you quit?" he asked her as they pulled into the underground garage she remembered from the night before.

To be honest, it had been easier to focus on Kenji breaking up with her than her part in the entire situation back then. They had been a good team, the top of their class, and worked well together. But it hadn't taken her long to realize that the life of an operative wasn't for her. When she entered law school and they formally started dating, he never asked her why she made the change. Just said that they'd be a different kind of team. And she'd thought, or rather hoped, that Kenji would continue his work and they'd be able to stay a couple.

Something she knew wasn't realistic, even at the

time. "That work wasn't for me. I was good, but I knew that you were better. And it was changing me... I didn't like it."

The tension didn't really leave his body. It was going to take him a while to come down from that drive. He was still wound up from everything that had happened at the museum. He needed time to think and process what was going on so he could find the patterns of their pursuer and then find whoever was after Daphne.

He'd parked the car, and she sat next to him, her hands held tightly in her lap. Why she'd left the training program that would have seen them both in the CIA hadn't been something he'd ever intended to inquire about, but she had been good. They had been good.

And although he knew he'd broken up with her because of the career he wanted for himself, another part of him knew that seeing her go in another direction had been a piece of it. He wanted to be immersed in the life of a CIA operative, and nothing was going to keep him from achieving that. Not even Daphne.

But all of that was a distraction. He knew what he needed. A fight or some kind of physical release, which just made him think about what she looked like when she came in his arms. And it had been so long that he'd have thought that memory would have faded, but it hadn't.

They were so close in the car, he couldn't breathe without inhaling the spicy sweet scent of her perfume. He undid his seat belt and then forced himself to put his hands back on the steering wheel. If he didn't, he was going to reach for Daphne, and he wasn't going to be able to let her go until he was buried deep inside her body.

Which probably wasn't what she needed right now.

Putting her first allowed him to grapple with his self-control and win for the moment.

"We need to call the cops and report the car tailing us. Also, I think we need to brainstorm about who is after you and start narrowing down the leads. My first priority is your safety, so if you can swing the time away from your office for the rest of the day, I'd like to stay here."

She undid her seat belt and twisted her body to face him. "Back to business."

"Yes. I shouldn't have asked you about why you left. That decision was your own, and you can't have any regrets given the career you've had and the people's lives you've made better."

He didn't want to go back to his own pain when she'd told him she had left the program. The confusion it had caused in him and the feelings of once again being left because of who he was. There wasn't anything healthy about that kind of thinking. Both of them had made choices, and their lives had taken them on their own paths. That was enough for Kenji.

"Sure. But what about us?"

"There would probably not have been an us even if you'd stayed and I hadn't broken up with you. The CIA isn't exactly about building trust in people or about making long-term bonds," he said dryly.

"Yeah. So let me check my schedule, and then I'll let you know about the rest of today," she said.

She pulled her phone out, and he watched her long,

manicured fingers moving on the screen, swiping to check her schedule and then tapping out a message.

"Okay. I've asked for the rest of the day off. Carl wants a call to discuss the latest attack on me. But I told him I needed some time to clean up, and then we could talk. Will that work?"

"Yes. I want to clear your entire staff before we go back to your office. Lee's had a day, so she should have most of them finished," Kenji said.

"A day? Is that long enough?"

They both got out of the car, and as they walked toward the elevator, she noticed Xander from the night before waiting there. The big guy had practically blended into the shadows.

"X, three bullets to the driver's window. I'm not sure if they put a tracer on the car. Lee's electronic security will mute any signal from getting out, but can you check it?" Kenji said, tossing the keys to Xander as they walked by him.

"No prob. You two okay?"

"Yes," Daphne said.

Kenji just nodded as they got on the elevator.

"How did my phone work?" Daphne asked since there was an electronic signal blocker in place.

"Last night, when I gave you access to the Wi-Fi, your device was registered as known, so it isn't blocked."

"Oh, wow. I had no idea something like that existed."

"Lee's got all sorts of tech that you probably don't want to know about," he said. "Do you want to get changed first and then talk to the team?"

"That would be nice," she said.

He noticed the stiff way she held herself with her

arms around her waist, and he hated that. Once again, the tension that he hadn't been able to shake was back. It was all he could do not turn pull her into his arms and hit the elevator stop button. He needed…hell, he was pretty sure he needed Daphne. He needed to hold her and make love to her. Reassure himself that she was safe.

He leaned slightly toward her and she leaned closer to him just as the elevator doors opened.

"Kenji, we need to talk."

Van waited as Kenji turned to him and stepped in front of Daphne.

"Of course. Let me get Daphne into my apartment."

Van just nodded.

"Take your time," Kenji said, opening the door to his apartment and motioning for Daphne to go inside.

Chapter 11

Kissing Kenji would have been a mistake—she knew that—but another part of her had needed it. It wasn't just everything that had happened today. It was everything that was going on in her life right now.

She ran her hands down the sides of her hips and couldn't help but feel dirty from being on the floor of the archives. Inside she was still trembling from the day. A hot shower and maybe a chance to lean against the wall and just let her guard down for a moment would be nice.

Kenji was doing his best to keep her safe, but she was still scared. Days of being attacked were starting to take a toll on her. This case wasn't nearly the most high-profile one she'd ever taken, and yet it was definitely the most dangerous.

She realized she was holding her breath as she walked to her room. Once she was inside it and the door closed behind her, she exhaled and wanted to scream but just quietly cried instead.

Stripping off her clothes, she walked naked to the bathroom and turned on the hot water before getting into the shower. She stood at the back of the cubicle and leaned her forehead against the tiled walls. Tears were easy enough to explain, and they didn't bother her. Men punched things. In her experience, women cried. It was just the way nature had made her, and she wasn't going to beat herself up for a normal reaction.

The tears passed as her mind started to force her to recover. It was something she'd learned to do as a child when she'd thought she'd done something that would impress her mother, but instead had been told to stop bragging about herself. There had been no way to make her mom proud, and Daphne wished she'd learned that at eight instead of ten years after her mom had died.

She tried to use that knowledge about herself in her work and everyday life to avoid repeating mistakes.

She heard the bedroom door open and knew that Kenji was in her room. He rapped on the bathroom door.

"Yes."

"Just wanted to let you know I'm in the apartment."

She opened her mouth to thank him, but instead his name came out.

"Yes?"

"I don't want to be alone," she said.

He didn't say anything, and she shook her head. If she'd learned anything from these last twenty-four hours with Kenji, it was that he wasn't going to compromise the job he'd been hired to do.

But then the door opened, and she saw him standing at the end of the nicely appointed bathroom through the glass wall of the shower cubicle.

He watched her for a minute, and she knew he was waiting for her to invite him further. She pushed the shower head so that it hit the wall and opened the door.

He took his clothes off.

She couldn't tear her eyes away as she watched him shrug out of his suit jacket and then slowly remove his tie. His fingers moved down the buttons of his shirt, and he shrugged out of it, tossing it on top of the growing pile of his clothes on the floor.

He toed off his shoes before he undid his pants and pushed them down his legs along with his underwear. Her breath caught in her throat as she really looked at all of him. His wide shoulders tapered to a lean but muscled chest and then a slim waist. His erection was large and strong.

It was undeniable. He wanted her as much as she wanted him.

Kenji bent to take off his socks and then stood, pushing his bangs back as he walked slowly toward her. She licked her lips as he stepped inside the shower, pulling her into his arms. Her body was wet and his was dry, and her breasts felt slick against the solidness of his chest. His hands were on her waist and then on her butt as he lifted her more fully into his body and lowered his head to kiss her.

His mouth was familiar to her now, his tongue against hers stirring a fire deep inside of her. There was a pulse of feminine heat between her legs as she felt his cock against her stomach. She put her arms around his shoulders and angled her head to deepen their kiss.

He turned so that he leaned against the wall and lifted her up with his hands on her hips. Then she parted her legs, wrapping them around his hips. She felt the tip of his penis first against her clit, which felt nice and sent a ripple through her.

She swallowed hard and shifted her body against

his until she felt him at her entrance. Their eyes met as she put her hands on his shoulders and slid down on his cock. She had missed him more than she'd allowed herself to admit until this moment. He turned so that her back was against the wall. His mouth was on her neck, kissing and sucking at her skin as he drove into her again and again.

She couldn't think of the past or the present. The danger she was in disappeared, and the world become just hers and Kenji's. She drove herself against him and felt that shiver in her center as her body started to tighten, and then her orgasm rushed over her. She bit his shoulder as she shuddered and came in his arms. He braced one hand against the wall by her head and drove up and into her again and again until he cried out her name and she felt his cock swell in her body. Then he came inside of her.

She held him, her head on his shoulder, the water still pounding around them. Neither of them spoke, but words would have only ruined this moment. Instead they washed each other silently and then exited the shower.

Kenji had promised his boss he'd get Daphne to the "war room," as they liked to call the big conference room they used when everyone was involved with one client. But he wasn't rushing this. He also wasn't rushing himself.

He'd waited too long to be back in her life to not take having her in his arms again seriously. He wrapped a towel around her and then pulled her close to him, hugging her, because he knew that this might have been a one-off moment.

She'd had a really rough day, and he wasn't ruling out the fact that she'd turned to him for some human contact and release to deal with the stress and tension.

Her head nestled on his shoulder felt right. Like she belonged back in his arms. Though a part of him wasn't entirely sure he'd be able to keep her there.

"Any regrets, Daph?"

The way he held her, she couldn't see his face, which was what he wanted. He was scared of her answer. Almost as much as he had been worried for her safety when she'd been turned around in the car seat to take photos while he'd been driving over one hundred miles per hour. But this time he had no skills to fall back on, no way of keeping his guard up if she said yes.

"No. You?"

"Definitely not."

He let out a relieved breath, which made her laugh as she stepped back. "Worried, were you?"

"Very. Clients get freaked when they've had a day like yours," he said.

She pulled her towel up higher and took a few more steps away from him. "Is this all part of the Kenji service?"

Fuck.

Of course he'd said the wrong thing. "No. That's not what I meant."

"What did you mean?" she asked, turning to the sink, where she'd left a bathrobe draped on the counter. She pulled it on and then dropped her towel, so he knew he'd hurt her.

God, this was hard. He understood what he had to say. If he wanted a second chance with her, he had to just lay it bare and talk about the emotions he had for her. But he felt raw and hated that.

"I like you. I have never slept with a client. I said that because I know what you're feeling might be motivated by fear and adrenaline. I'm more used to being shot at and chased than you are, and even I'm a little shaken."

She turned then, running her brush through her hair, but he noticed that she wasn't glaring at him anymore.

"*Shaken* is a good word to use. Today has been a lot. But I'm not a woman to just sleep with a man to release tension."

"I shouldn't have worded it the way I did," he said. "I still suck at that."

"You do," she agreed.

He smiled at her. "Truce?"

"Truce."

"I'll leave you to finish up. We can discuss next steps over lunch, and then Van is calling in the available team to strategize in the conference room if you're up for it."

"Yeah, I'll be there. I want to be involved in all discussions and planning," she said.

"I knew you would."

He bent to pick up his clothes from the floor and noticed her watching him in the mirror as he stood back up. But she didn't say anything, and he hesitated for a second before nodding at her and walking out the door.

She had her suitcase on the bed, and he noted she had a journal on her nightstand as well as a book. He couldn't read the title but was curious which book she'd taken from his library. He didn't like dust jackets, so he'd removed them all, and the hardcover was just a brown color.

He would ask her about it later. Hooking up with Daphne had felt right in the moment, but Kenji had realized at the museum and in the car that he wanted more with her than just this assignment. He'd be lying if he said he hadn't from the moment her name had come up in the briefing.

He walked through the living area of his apartment and into his bedroom, putting his clothes in the laundry bag and then quickly getting dressed in another black suit, white shirt and thin black tie. He snapped on his holster, tied his shoes, and went back into the other room as his phone pinged, letting him know that the lunch he'd ordered was being brought up by Van.

His boss was hovering, and Kenji wasn't sure why. Was Kenji giving something away about his feelings for Daphne? Or was it just that this case should have been a lot simpler than it was turning out to be?

He opened the door when Van arrived.

"You're not usually the delivery guy," Kenji said.

"No, I'm not."

"Why?"

Van came into the apartment and put the food on the counter. He leaned against it, his legs crossed at the ankles. So this wasn't going to be a quick convo.

"Just wanted to make sure you both were okay. Those shots in the window were aimed right at your head," Van said.

Kenji hadn't allowed himself to dwell on that. The shooter had meant to kill him, maybe with the intent to kidnap Daphne. Something that Kenji wasn't going to let happen.

"Yeah, that's why I came right here. We need to figure out what's going on."

"I agree. Lee's almost done with all the info you asked her to pull on Daphne's work colleagues. I brought up a file you might want to check out and talk to her about privately."

Great. That meant someone on her staff had raised a red flag.

"Thanks."

Van nodded and then left. Kenji glanced down at the file that Van had handed him and realized it was for the paralegal who'd gotten freaked out on the first day. Alan Field. He was related to Pierce Lauder.

Daphne dried her hair and then got dressed, taking her time with her makeup because she always felt stronger when she looked her best. It was a bit of her faking confidence, but once she had her pantsuit on and her heels, she felt like the successful attorney she was.

Not the woman who'd just cuddled in her lover's arms, trying to recover from one of the hardest days she'd ever experienced. She wasn't about to start unpacking her emotions about what had happened between the two of them. Not now. She wanted to figure out why someone was coming so hard after her.

She needed to return the censer she'd found, which she thought was her top priority. Kenji had mentioned that his boss would have the cops come here to collect it. Maybe having it in police custody would stop the attacks on her.

Maybe wasn't her favorite word because it usually meant no. But this time she wasn't sure. Walking out into the living room, she noticed that Kenji had set up the table and was waiting for her.

"What's for lunch?" she asked.

She wondered why he always wore the black suit. It looked good on him, and maybe he used it like she did as armor for his day. She wasn't going to ask him, but she was curious.

"Cobb salad with blue cheese dressing."

Her favorite. It mattered to her that he'd remember that tiny detail. "Thank you."

He shrugged as if it were nothing, but it wasn't. It showed her that leaving her back then…it almost made her feel better about it. His words had started to heal that broken, hurt part that still lingered inside of her, but this…was helping too.

She sat down, setting her phone and notebook next to her spot. Kenji sat across from her. She started to eat and then noticed he wasn't touching his lunch.

"What is it?"

"There is a connection between one of your paralegals and the museum," Kenji said carefully, then turned the electronic tablet next to his spot toward her.

She put her fork down as she saw that it was Alan. He'd been doing a lot of the leg work on this case for her. He'd been the one to do all of the research for the brief she'd used to ask the judge to compel the museum to give her access to their archives and inventory.

"How is he connected to the museum?"

He could be a donor and maybe have a relative on the board. Maybe it wasn't as bad as her mind was making it.

"He's Pierce Lauder's nephew."

Nope. It was definitely a connection that she couldn't ignore. "Okay. I'll need to speak to him. I know we said I'd stay here today, but I think this can't wait."

"I agree. We can head to your office after lunch," Kenji said.

"Yes. Did your boss talk to the cops about me turning over the censer?" she asked.

"He did, and they will be here around four this afternoon. Originally you were meant to be at your office."

"I know. That's good. I was thinking perhaps the attacks on me might stop if the censer is known to be with the cops," Daphne said.

"That's a nice thought."

"Don't be placating. You sound fake," she said.

He shrugged and tipped his head to the left. "It was meant to be supportive."

She took another bite of her salad, but she wasn't sure she could enjoy it. Her mind was buzzing with the thought that Alan might be feeding Pierce information on their case. She was trying to make a connection to one solid piece of evidence, but nothing was coming to her. She wanted to blame the day and was going to.

Because otherwise it meant that she'd trusted the wrong person. She thought she'd become so much better about that than she apparently had. "I wonder why we didn't catch that when he was hired and assigned to my team."

"Were you representing your client then?" Kenji asked.

"No. In fact, he came on to work on a human rights case. He's been one of my most reliable paralegals," she said.

"He might still be. There's a connection. It might not be more than a blood relation that he never talks to," Kenji said.

He had a point. She could have worked for her mom's rival law firm and nothing would have passed between the two of them. "I just hate that you found anything on the people on my staff."

"I hate it too," he said.

"But you expected it?"

He leaned forward, and that fall of bangs drifted away from his face until he pushed it back up on his head. "I did. Somehow your movements are known to whoever is attacking you."

"They did follow us when we left."

"Yes, which means maybe your paralegal isn't leaking your whereabouts. Or, as you said, they just want the censer back."

She thought about that for a minute, rubbing her shoulder where it still hurt, remembering the soft kisses that Kenji had dropped on it when they'd both been washing. She thought back to the drive to the Price Security building and realized something she'd missed before.

The shots fired at the car had been aimed at Kenji's head. The shooter had been trying to take him out.

Looking up to find him concentrating on her, she cleared her throat. "Do you think they want to kidnap me?"

He rubbed the back of his neck and then looked her straight in the eyes. "It would seem that way based on the car."

"What am I going to do?"

"Exactly what we've discussed. My buddy Xander just got hired on as security in your office building, and he'll make sure your office is secure before I bring you in."

Chapter 12

She wore a slim-fitting black sweater that hugged her curves and drew his eyes to her breasts. It was short-sleeved again, which just showed off her toned arms. The sling and bandage had been removed from her shoulder now, and he saw her move her arm gingerly, testing the movement.

She walked to the table to collect her yellow handbag. It matched the flowers appliqued on her brown knee-length skirt. The large yellow blooms ran down the left side. She had on those high heels again.

"Kenji?"

"Hmm."

"You're staring at my legs."

"Just wondering how you can walk in those heels," he said quickly, tearing his eyes from them and forcing his gaze up to her face. She was clearly amused and saw through his smoke screen.

She winked and said, "Very carefully."

Flirting. She was *flirting* with him, and he wanted to flirt back, but he knew that he was walking a very difficult line. He needed to keep her safe. With each passing day and the time they spent together, it was getting harder and harder for him to do just that.

"I'm impressed," he said, before pivoting away from her and leading the way down to the car.

She was quiet as they drove back to her office in a brand-new vehicle. There hadn't been a tracker on the damaged one. Kenji wasn't really sure if that was a good thing or not. It made him feel like they weren't dealing with a professional. The attacks on Daphne had been sporadic, and they had been more menacing than lethal in his estimation. Not that having her house broken into and ransacked hadn't been harrowing for Daphne, but there didn't seem to be any real skill behind the attacker.

Even the car following them earlier in the day had been too aggressive, not a trained operative. Which worried him. Amateurs made mistakes that professionals didn't. But the shooter had been steady so possibly a pro. Daphne's shoulder injury might have been a warning or just a bad shot. At first he'd thought it was a warning, but the incident in the archives had the feel of someone who was just pissed off rather than any real menace. Though the coffee mug would have concussed Daphne if she'd been hit with it.

"Do you remember where Grey was standing when you two were talking?" he asked.

"What?"

"I'm trying to replay the mug hitting the wall in my head, and it's not clear if the mug was aimed at you or her," Kenji said.

"She was already out the door when the mug came. It was aimed at me," she said. "I looked up at the wall from where you'd pushed me down, and there were fragments in front of my eyes."

Damn.

"So the bookcases that were pushed over might have been a warning to Grey that her partner was there."

"Yes. But why not use a gun?" Daphne asked.

"I'm not sure. Maybe they meant to but didn't have time," he said. "Did it seem that Grey was about to tell you something?"

Kenji had been only half paying attention to the actual conversation. He hadn't liked the room with the tall rows of bookshelves that offered ample hiding places.

"I believe she was," Daphne said.

Which didn't really help him that much. "What if she'd been meant to tell you one thing and instead deviated?"

Daphne closed her eyes, and he had the feeling that she was reliving the moment in her head. "She was nervous and didn't like that I called her out on being the person who'd contacted me. Maybe her partner didn't know that?"

"Yes, and if they overheard your questioning, they'd know that Grey had spoken to you. Maybe the bookcase was to shut her up before she gave you the name?"

Daphne pulled out her notebook and made a few notes. "I think you might be right. Will Lee be able to find her?"

"Even if she goes to ground, Lee will find her. It might take a few days, but she'll get Grey Joy for us."

"Good. I need to talk to her. Now I'm wondering what she was going to tell me about the items. Clearly someone at the museum wanted her to give me information that would help their side of the case."

"How?" Kenji asked.

"I'm not sure. It seems the missing items are the key,

but I do wonder if I should be concentrating on them. The already known items, though, are really not enough to satisfy my client. She wants all of them returned."

Kenji didn't understand the legalities and what the different pieces meant culturally or monetarily to her client. "Do you know the value of the missing pieces?"

"I have the museum's figures, which Marjorie accepted as factual. And there is no pattern to the money. I might try to go talk to the great-grandson of the man who took the items originally. They were labeled spoils of war, so he was able to legally keep them at the time. But the museum has mismatched records on what was donated, and it doesn't line up with what my client believes they have or some photos I saw of an exhibit as recently as 2015."

He liked listening to her talk about the case as she continued telling him about the inconsistencies and how she was going to ferret out the truth. She also stopped looking so white and nervous when she discussed the details of the case and getting justice for her client. He liked the changes he saw in her. The woman he'd known when they'd been in college had this same fire, but it seemed honed now. Her intelligence had always been there, and she used it to make connections and rule out possibilities.

He had the feeling she'd leave no stone unturned to get a winning result for her client. Which he appreciated. "Send me the donor's name if you don't mind. We can run down his information for you."

"I was going to have my team… I guess you're right. Until I talk to Alan and the rest of them, I really don't know who to trust. And I don't want to put anyone else in danger," she said.

He liked that she was thinking now about her safety in a way she hadn't been last night when she'd gone into the alleyway by herself. Once that feeling of security everyone enjoyed had been ripped away from her, she wasn't going to trust again easily.

He hit his earpiece as they pulled into the parking garage for her law firm and let Xander know they were there.

"Garage and elevator secure. Lee is looped in with closed circuit cameras that Rick and I installed. You're clear to Daphne's office," Xander said.

Kenji relayed that to Daphne before they both got out of the car and he escorted her to her temporary office. She put her purse in her desk and then asked to have the paralegal brought in to see her.

"Where do you want me?"

"By the door, I guess. I wish I was in my office. It's more intimidating than this closet you put me in."

"You're plenty intimidating without the big office," he said.

Daphne always tried to approach her work like justice itself. Blind to everything but the facts, and usually she could succeed in keeping her emotions out of it. But there were some cases where it was harder. She usually didn't struggle with that in the workplace, yet there were days.

Today was one of those days. She let Alan sweat as he sat in the guest chair that Kenji had brought in for him. A part of her brain was busy mechanically listing all the reasons why he might have concealed the fact that he was related to Pierce Lauder. The other part of her was too hurt to care.

She trusted everyone on her team to want the same results. A win for their client of course meant prestige within the firm and a chance for promotion or partner, depending on their position, so that was always a factor too. But this was different. Alan should have recused himself the moment he learned that his uncle was a named codefendant in the case.

"I'm not sure why I'm here," Alan said, clearly nervous.

"Alan, I'm going to ask you something, and I want you to be honest," Daphne said, taking her time to make sure she could be calm. Maybe if it didn't feel like a personal betrayal it would have been easier, but it did.

"Of course," Alan said, leaning forward. "Daphne, I wouldn't lie to you about anything."

"Are you related to Pierce Lauder?" she asked. Because that was clearly a lie by omission.

He turned beet-red, licked his lips, then swallowed. "You know I am."

"I do. What I don't know is why you never disclosed that relationship and if you are feeding him information," she said.

"I'd never do that. My uncle and I aren't close. In fact, I haven't seen him since I was twelve. He and my mom had a falling out," Alan said.

Daphne didn't want to hear about his family's drama. Everyone had their own version of it. Someone got upset by someone else, and they didn't talk for years. Or they had her version of family drama. Where one person didn't like another one and ignored them, and the rest of the family ignored it as if they couldn't see the damage. Whoa, she thought. She wasn't unpacking that in the office with Alan and Kenji.

She was tired, which was the only excuse she could come up with for all these memories of her mother. And she'd been alive when Kenji and Daphne had been together the last time. Not that that mattered right now.

"That's your mom's relationship with him. Why didn't you say anything to me?"

He rubbed the back of his neck and then scooted forward in his chair toward her. Kenji moved subtly toward Alan.

But he didn't need to. Alan's face was earnest. "I didn't know how. I took a job here because of men like my uncle who put the reputation of their collection above the rightful owners of the pieces they exhibit. I wanted to work here to help right that wrong. I never expected this case to come to us or that it would be you who got it."

"Fair enough, but once I did, you should have mentioned it," she said.

"I was going to, but you were giving me a lot of work to do. No ego here, but I am really good at research and pulling together precedent. I liked the work. Once you were shot, I knew I had to mention it, but you haven't been available on your own," he said.

"You're good at what you do, and I feel the same way about cases that are handed to me. But I have had to recuse myself from more than one," she said. "I hated to do it, but it was the right thing to do."

She'd recused herself from a case that would have seen her go up against her own mother in court. Daphne had struggled with that decision because there was nothing she wanted more than to beat her mom. But she'd known that she couldn't be unbiased when it came to any case involving her mom. Was it the same for Alan?

She wasn't entirely sure that trusting him was a smart decision, but she also didn't see any malintent in him. Glancing up at Kenji, she saw him shake his head. He wasn't sure she could trust Alan still.

"Where were you today?"

"I've been in the office all morning, working on the case. I talked to the new security guy for a while," Alan said.

"What did you discuss?"

Alan looked sheepish. "*Halo.* We both play it online."

Kenji's face changed, and he gave her a small nod. She guessed that Xander had already been checking Alan out, which she wasn't too pleased with. But it did show her how much her safety meant not just to Kenji but to the entire Price Security team.

"For now I'm going to allow you to remain on the case," Daphne said. "From this point forward, there can be no contact with Pierce Lauder. If he contacts you, let me know immediately."

"Thank you, Daphne. I will. I don't think he'll call me or anything. He doesn't have my number."

"I'm glad to hear that. That's all for now."

Kenji opened the door, and Alan got up and left her office. After the door closed, Kenji leaned back against it, and she remembered how he'd stood in the doorway of the bathroom earlier. A sensual shiver went through her.

Like she needed to be thinking about sex right now.

"So, your buddy checked Alan out?"

"I didn't know that. As soon as we arrived back at the tower, Van let me know about Alan, and I let you know. I assume that Van thought he was a security risk and wanted to check it out before you were back in the office."

"I appreciate it, but next time, I want to be looped in before it happens," she said.

"Yes, ma'am."

He was being all formal and agreeable, but she knew that he'd do whatever he felt was in her best interests, even if it ticked her off.

Daphne had a meeting with her boss that Kenji followed her to, sort of like a silent shadow. That was how he always liked to think of himself when he was on the job. Moving in tandem with his client to keep them safe but not to intrude on their lives. The struggle with Daphne was different than with other clients because he cared about her. Deeply.

But he'd been aware of that when he'd agreed to take the case. He wasn't sure what he'd expected. Getting into his feelings had never been easy for him, and this time wasn't any different. It was harder because the only woman he'd truly ever loved was his mom, and she'd died shortly after he'd gone to college.

Kenji'd reacted with an afternoon of deep grieving and then shoved the rest of his emotions down and kept them locked away. He hadn't known how to process that, and at the time, he hadn't been going to therapy. The sessions he had with his therapist mainly dealt with his father.

"I want you to think seriously of coming off this case,

Daphne. I know you've done all the legwork. At this point, if we let Sam take over, she'll just get it over the finish line for you," Carl said. "Your life means more than this win."

Daphne made herself even stiffer and taller, if that were possible. "I have a bodyguard, and I think stepping back now would just signal that whoever is intimidating me is succeeding. Who's to say Sam would be safe?"

Carl leaned back in the big leather chair that he sat in, glancing over at Kenji. Kenji held himself still in the ready position. Van had worked with Carl before, so the other man knew that Kenji was the best in the business. "What do you think? Can you keep her safe?"

"Yes, sir."

Kenji understood where Carl was coming from. No one wanted to see one of their employees threatened and injured. But the cases that Daphne's firm represented often put them in the line of fire. They were human rights cases that won the hearts of the public but often not those of the defendants on the other side.

"What can I do to help?" he asked.

"I know that Ben Cross has filed a motion to delay the trial again this morning. We've filed a counter-motion, but if you could talk to Judge Mallon's office, it might help," Daphne said. "I feel like all of these attacks must mean that the evidence I've compelled them to present is more damning than they want us to know."

"But we don't know why?" Carl asked.

"Not yet. I'm trying to talk with the man who donated the entire cache that is at the heart of my case. I think there must be a connection I'm just not seeing yet. The missing items on the inventory… I feel like someone, maybe Lauder, knows exactly where they are. The archivist I was speaking to was about to reveal something when we were attacked," Daphne said.

"I trust your instincts, which is why I assigned this case to you. I'll talked to Mallon's office and stressed that we don't want any more delays." Carl turned to him. "Do you believe the threat to Daphne will be lessened after the case goes to court?"

"Oh, definitely. They are trying to keep her from finding out something," Kenji said.

"Good. I'll add that in as well. Maybe see if I can get it moved up," Carl said. "Keep me in the loop with the evidence. Will you be talking to the archivist again?"

"Definitely. I'm waiting to hear back from her," Daphne said.

Kenji knew that was a white lie, but also that his team would find Grey Joy, and Daphne would have the chance to talk to her.

Carl and Daphne wrapped up their conversation, and they left his office. In the hall, as they headed toward the elevator, he was alert, watching for anyone. But knowing that Xander and Rick had installed closed circuit cameras made him less anxious than he had been yesterday when he'd come into her office.

"That went better than expected," Daphne said when they got on the elevator and were alone.

"I always knew you'd get a result," he said.

"You did? How?"

He looked over at her. "You don't fail when you put your mind to something. Ever. Carl was always going to come around to your way of thinking because he knows that as well."

"You make me sound…"

"Awesome," he said simply.

She shook her head. "I'm not, but thank you. Between Carl and Alan, it's been a day, and I still have to hand over the censer to the cops later. I would like to do some work and try again to reach John Hazelton-Measham so that I can set up an appointment, and I need to talk to my team and let them know about Alan."

"Whatever you need," he said. He'd already made sure the conference room where she liked to work with her team was as secure as he could make it. He settled into the corner of the room where he had a clear view of the door and Daphne as she worked.

He noticed how everyone on her team worked at a very high level, which he knew was down to Daphne. She gave her all, so everyone around her did the same.

When they were alone in the conference room as she wrapped up her day, he couldn't help watching her—not as her bodyguard, but as a man observing a woman he cared deeply about. The emotions were there, and he was afraid to name them at this moment, but that didn't mean he wasn't feeling them.

Chapter 13

One last thing, she thought, and then she could lie in her bed and pretend she was going to sleep. When they got back to Price Security, Van let them know that Detective Miller was waiting in the conference room. Daphne retrieved the censer from the safe. Legally she probably should have surrendered this as soon as she was conscious in the hospital, but she hoped the officer would be understanding.

Her shoulder was at a dull ache, but only because she'd forgotten about the injury and slung her work bag over that shoulder. Kenji was taking a break, and his coworker, Luna Urban, was with her as she went to talk to the cop.

Luna had introduced herself earlier but had just quietly stood in the background. Unlike with Kenji, Daphne didn't really notice the woman who was acting as her bodyguard. When they got into the conference room, she did notice that Van Price was in the corner on his device. The muscled bald man looked intimidating to her for the first time. The expression on his face was tense and almost menacing.

But when he heard them enter, he looked up, his face softening into a smile. "Good evening, ladies."

He walked over to them, and she noted the angel wings tattoo on the back of his neck as he gave Luna a one-armed hug. "We don't see this one much anymore."

"That's only because Jaz wanted me on tour again, and Nick missed me while I was gone," Luna said.

The names meant nothing to Daphne, who just smiled and moved toward the cop while the other two caught up.

Detective Miller was short and had brown curly hair streaked with gray. She wore a dark blue suit and a button-down white blouse. She had her badge clipped to her belt and a shoulder holster that Daphne first noticed when she shrugged out of her jacket. Her nails were short and neat on one hand, but the thumbnail on her left hand had been chewed back to the quick.

Daphne guessed her job wasn't without its stresses. She pulled a pair of reading glasses from her shoulder bag and put them on. When she looked up, Daphne realized her eyes were a gorgeous light blue, and she had thick eyelashes.

Her voice when she spoke had an air of authority to it that she'd also noticed in Officer Martinez's voice the other night. Most cops she'd worked with over the years had it. They knew they had to be calm but also project it to the person they were interrogating.

Daphne wasn't planning on being anything but honest with the detective. It wouldn't help Daphne find out how the censer had ended up in an alley if she wasn't honest. Working with the courts, she knew she should have turned it in much sooner, but she wasn't going to fabricate a date when she got it to make herself look better. Right now, the only way she was going to find answers was to be as honest as she could.

And being honest with the detective was easier than being honest with herself about her currently messy feelings where Kenji was concerned.

"Thank you for coming down here," she said after they'd introduced themselves. "I found this the night I was shot and put it in my bag. I was finally able to look at it yesterday. As soon as I did, I recognized it as an item that was marked missing in my current legal case. Things...have been hectic."

"That's putting it mildly. Van caught me up on everything that has happened to you. I'm happy to take your statement and this item into custody," Detective Miller said. "I assume today was the first moment you had to turn it in."

"It was," Daphne said.

"If there is anything to be investigated, we will look into it."

"Sorry. That sounded like I was telling you how to do your job. It's just...never mind. Do you have a statement form for me to fill out?" she asked the detective.

"I do. And I'd also like to record your statement as well. I will notify the museum that we have found an item of theirs."

Daphne gave her story. When they were done recording it and she'd signed her written statement, Daphne lingered.

"Yes?" Detective Miller said.

"The censer is a sacred tabot for the Ethiopian Orthodox Church. I'm not sure of the way it should be handled, but the way I found it shows no respect for the church or its believers."

"I'll see if we can contact someone from the church to make sure it's handled properly."

"Thank you. I know it is the property of the Los Angeles Museum of Foreign Cultures, but it had been marked missing and not stolen as recently as yesterday. Would you mind checking to see if any other items similar to this have been turned in?"

"That's not my job, but I can send you some paperwork to fill out so that the evidence clerk can do a search. I am interested in this idea of missing but not stolen. Are there any stolen items on the list?"

Daphne pulled it out. "No, but one of my paralegals found two of the missing items listed for sale on a black market art website. I think this item that I found might be the key to locating these other ones."

"Were you able to purchase the missing items?" the detective asked.

"No. In fact, we can no longer access the site at all. I have two screen grabs that aren't the highest quality," Daphne said.

"Send them to me and include them in your evidence request. I work in homicide, so I can't take this case, but I'll see it gets to the right hands."

"If you work in homicide, why are you here?" she asked.

"Van asked me, and I owed him a favor," she said. "Where can I reach you?"

Daphne gave the detective her cell phone number, and then the detective left. Van came over to her and sat down next to her. "I overheard you mention the black market. I think Lee can help with that. Do you have the URL for the site?"

"Just from the screen grab," she said. "It's not clear. We had clicked on a photo that matched a description of one of the items."

"Do you have time now?" Van asked. "I'd like to get your entire missing list to Lee so she can start digging around for you. Especially if you think they might be going to auction."

"I do have time." She knew she wasn't going to sleep, and she'd much rather get the answers she needed. If Carl was successful at getting their court date moved up, she'd have something substantial to take into court.

It was beginning to look to her like maybe the reason talks had broken down between her client and the museum was that they were doing something shady with the disputed items. She still wasn't clear what the actual play they were making was, but she felt like she was getting much closer to finding some answers.

She spent the next two hours in the computer room with Lee, impressed by the way the woman pulled information together. She was keenly intelligent, and Daphne would love to have someone like her on her team, which she mentioned.

"I can't leave Price Security, but if you need an assist, I'm always available," she said.

"Thanks." Daphne said goodbye to Lee and walked out of the office to find Kenji waiting for her.

She was happy to see him and started to reach for him to hug him, but he stopped her. He put his hand on the small of her back and directed her toward the elevator at the end of the hall.

* * *

The sun was setting as they walked out of her office to his car. Kenji was on alert. Even knowing that Xander and Rick had installed extra security measures didn't ease the tension in his gut. It was bringing back memories of his last assignment in Afghanistan before he'd retired from the CIA.

All of his instincts told him they were being watched. When they got to the car, instead of opening the door for Daphne, he kept her between his body and the vehicle.

"What is it?" she asked. She held her shoulder bag closer to her body.

"Someone is watching us," he said. "I want you to get in the car, lock the doors. The glass is bulletproof, but if there are shots fired at the car, leave. Drive to Price Security. The garage will open automatically for you."

"I'm not leaving you behind," she said.

"I don't have time to debate this. The light is good for this kind of hunt with the sun almost down. Do what I've asked." He opened the door and all but shoved her inside, tossing his keys on her lap.

She stopped him from closing the door.

He waited.

"Be careful."

He just nodded. He tapped his earpiece and pulled his weapon from his holster as he moved in the direction of one of the side buildings. From an earlier survey, he knew that it was a maintenance shed used by the lawn crew for the property.

"Wada here. I'm on the move. Someone is watching us."

"Got you. Where is Daphne?" Lee responded immediately.

"In the car with orders to go to Price Tower if things get hot," Kenji said. "Going silent."

"Affirmative. Sending backup," Lee said.

Kenji had learned early that missions depended on him. He relied on his team, but he had to be able to handle it by himself. He often thought of those old Western and martial arts movies him mom used to watch where a lone warrior had to defend a small village or town. That was how he saw himself.

He was tired of the game that was being played with Daphne. It was as if whoever was watching her was toying with her. He moved around the outbuilding to a small stand of trees that had been planted and was neatly manicured. He kept low as he ran.

There was a rustle in the leaves behind him. He turned as a man dressed in camo fired three shots in rapid succession at him. Kenji swerved his body to avoid being hit and dropped to the ground when the last one almost grazed his head. He watched as the assailant ran away from the building.

Kenji pushed himself off the ground and took off after him. The landscape in LA was hilly, rough terrain, and this part was no different. Kenji's suit was cut to allow him to pursue anyone. His shoes, though looking like fancy dress shoes, had a solid sole good for running. But the deepening shadows as the sun continued to set made it hard for him to find footing. He pursued the shooter down the side of the hill, and as he was getting close, he heard the sound of a car engine.

He slid to a stop at the edge of a paved road that

looked like it wasn't used frequently as the car pulled away. He got the make and model, but it didn't have a tag.

Kenji started to line up a shot but knew he wouldn't be able to hit it and never wasted bullets, so he reluctantly put his weapon back in the holster.

"Wada here. I pursued a shooter down to… Lee, can you get a GPS fix on my location?"

"Yes. Got it. You need extraction?"

"No, there was a late model Toyota Prius waiting. No tag. Looked like black or a dark blue color."

"I'll put an alert out for it. Xander is with Daphne. Do you want me to send them to you?"

"I need to check the shooter's nest. He wasn't a sniper, so he could have left a clue," Kenji said. "Might take me a few to get back up the hill."

"I'll let Xander know. Confirm when you are there."

Kenji hated that the other person got away. He reviewed his performance, looking for any errors. Today at the museum, after the attack, he'd noticed that his senses had been more attuned to Daphne, and the danger to her was secondary.

Was he putting her at risk by staying on this case?

Should he ask to be removed?

There was no easy answer. He wouldn't let anything happen to her. He knew he'd give his own life before he let her be hurt again. But was he sharp enough?

He had done better this evening, but it had been watching her interrogate Alan that had caused the shift in him. Seeing Daphne's passion and commitment to her case had made him realize that nothing was going to stop her from getting the case to court. That meant Kenji had to find and eliminate the threat to her.

There was no other solution at this point.

He got to the top of the hill and found where the watcher had been. There was an indentation from the body, but nothing else. No trash or cigarette butts.

Xander moved the car over to where Kenji was and got out to help him search.

"Daphne is ticked at you."

"Thanks. Use some of that SAS survival training and make sure I'm not missing anything," Kenji said. "I think he was between your height and mine. With the sun almost down, it was hard to get a look at him as we were running. He wasn't a good shot."

"That's positive. Daphne saw you hit the ground and called Van, and he sent me," Xander said.

"I get it. She's not happy with what I did, but it's my job to keep her safe, not make her feel great," he said.

Xander put his hand on Kenji's shoulder. "I know, mate. I just didn't want you walking in blind."

He took a deep breath, and that coil of tension in his gut was tighter than before. "Thanks."

Watching Kenji hit the ground as he ran across the parking lot wasn't something she could get out of her head. She'd forgotten what his job was and how his life had changed since they'd been together. Sleeping with him had opened up a part of her that she'd thought she'd said goodbye to. The part that wanted a partner and a family. But the reality of what Kenji did had been driven home when he'd locked her in the car and put himself right in the path of danger to protect her.

He was okay. Xander had told her that. He'd been scared when he'd driven into the parking lot at top speed and then expertly swung his vehicle next to hers, a little like he'd seen too many *Fast & Furious* movies. He'd gotten out of the Dodge Charger that was identical to the one she was sitting in. He came over to her, and she scooted to the passenger's side, unlocking the door so he could get in, which he did.

"Where is Kenji?" she asked.

"In pursuit of the shooter. That's all I know," Xander said.

His voice was calm and level with a British accent, which surprised her. She realized she hadn't really spoken to him before this. Just seen him. A big, muscled giant of a man who Kenji counted as a friend. That she did know, because of how Kenji spoke of the other man and how he acted around him.

Her throat felt tight, and she realized she'd much rather be with Kenji than sitting in the car waiting for him to get back. What if he was shot and injured? What if…

"Thanks for coming."

"No problem. The boss said you weren't exactly acting."

"I wasn't. Do you think you should go and help Kenji?" she asked. "I did ask for backup for him. I'm good in this car."

"Nah, he's fine," Xander said. "Actually, he's just checked in."

He caught her up on everything that had happened and told her Kenji would be making his way to their location.

Everyone was so calm. Which she guessed was how they needed to be. It wouldn't do for a security company to panic, but she hated how everyday this was for Xander and Van when she'd spoken to him.

It wasn't helping that she realized how much she cared for Kenji. These last two days had been intense, and she was being shoved into a place where there was no more room for subterfuge and pretending. No place to hide and act like the life she'd created for herself was fulfilling away from work. Or had been until Kenji had walked through the door and made her remember she was a woman and had at one time dreamed of a different life.

But the man Kenji was today…scared her. Or maybe not him, but the world he lived in. The world that would demand he give it his all. That world wasn't one she and he could exist in as a couple.

His reasons for breaking up with her still mattered almost fifteen years later. She'd somehow thought that they had changed. That since he wasn't CIA anymore, his life would be calmer. But tonight had showed her that it wasn't.

And she knew that her own life wasn't calm right now. Someone was threatening her, which was the reason he was in danger. But if he wasn't guarding her, he'd be guarding someone else.

"He's back. I'm going to move the car over so we can provide light for him to search the shooter's nest."

Just like that, he was back. She wasn't entirely sure she was ready to see and talk to him. "I need you to stay in the car. We believe the threat has passed but can't take any chances."

"Sure. I'll sit here while maybe the both of you are in danger."

"That's why your company hired us," Xander said in a very low and patient tone. "He's okay."

"Great."

Xander got out, and she caught her first glimpse of Kenji in the headlights of the car. His suit was dirty, and there was a rip above his right knee. He glanced in her direction and then turned away. Her heart was beating so fast she had to do some deep breathing exercises to calm herself down.

She knew that there was nothing she could do to change Kenji and that if she let herself fall for him again, the danger was going to be part of her life. As if she had any control over who she fell in love with. It was one thing to say that she wasn't going to allow herself to feel anything, but she'd never been one to lie to herself.

Well, there had been the one lie that if she changed everything about herself, her mom would love her. But she'd learned from that. She couldn't change for Kenji, and she'd never ask him to change for her.

He and Xander made a thorough search of the area before they both approached the car. They talked for a few more minutes, and then Xander loped off at a run toward his own Dodge as Kenji opened the door to get behind the wheel.

She had a million things she wanted to say to him. She wanted to yell at him for scaring her. She wanted to demand he tell her what he'd been thinking. Wanted to make him give her all the details and let her know if the danger he'd put himself in was worth it.

But then he turned toward her. Her mind stopped, and her heart took over. She threw herself in his arms, and he hugged her tightly to him. Neither of them saying a word.

Chapter 14

They drove down Wilshire on the way back to Price Tower. It seemed like Christmas as the lights were now out on the light poles. "I'm not ready for Christmas. I don't think my case is going to be done before it."

"I'm not either," Kenji said. "But I'm not really big into it."

"You mentioned that. My dad sends me a present, but we don't always get together," she said, rambling because she was really in her feelings right now, and she didn't like it.

"That's nice," he said.

The conversation felt stilted, like she was working too hard to talk to him. "I can't handle your life, Kenji. I just had no idea about the reality of watching you go after someone. When he fired at you and you hit the ground… I thought you were dead for a second, and a part of me wanted to die too."

He pulled the car off the road in the parking lot of a chain restaurant that was busy, and he drove it into a spot where he could watch the road and the entire lot. "It's not always like that."

She shook her head. "I appreciate what you are saying. But for a minute today, I think I was fooling myself into believing that when my case went to court and there wasn't a need for you to protect me, we might be able to see each other."

He put his hand on the steering wheel and shifted so he faced her. "I want that. Can we talk about this back at the tower? You're not safe here."

"We can talk, but I don't see a way forward for us. You're always going to be looking for danger and putting yourself in front of it. You're a protector, and I get and respect that. It's one of the things I really like about you, but I don't know if I can live with the fear I felt."

"You felt that fear because you're tired, and your own life is in danger. Let's get home, and we can talk about it when I'm not trying to watch the parking lot, okay? Don't write me off yet, Daphne."

"Of course. Let's get back there."

She hadn't meant to bring that up, but the fact was, her mind kept replaying him falling to the ground. She knew he was fine, but what if he hadn't been? The training she'd had was a lifetime ago, and she wasn't sure she could have done anything to help. Work. She needed to focus on the case.

Which she did now. "Do you know if Lee found the address for the donor of the items? My team hasn't found his current address. They think he might be in a care home."

"You don't have to stop talking to me about us," he said.

"There is no us, Kenji, is there? We both had some unresolved stuff from the past, but it's my case that brought you back into my life. So I need to focus on that."

Even as she talked, she knew that she wasn't as clear-headed as she needed to be. This case had been difficult from the beginning. Her client had come to her as a last resort. Marjorie had been working with a number of museums around the world to get the items originally taken during the siege back to her country. And everyone was willing to continue the discussion and was on good terms until recently, when the Los Angeles Museum of Foreign Cultures had started blocking her attempts to see them.

"I'm not done with this discussion. Yes, my job is dangerous, but it's nothing compared to what I used to do. To be fair, this is the first time I've been shot at in like seven months."

Seven months without someone firing at him. "That must feel like forever for you."

"It does. When I was still an operative, it happened a lot more frequently. There were people I couldn't protect, lives that were lost, and this job gives me a chance to save some."

She realized that she'd touched a nerve with her comment and reminded herself she wasn't the only one who had feelings here. "I'm sorry that you lost people."

"It's part of the job, and we all knew the risk. That's why I got out. I want to use the skills I've honed to save lives and keep people safe. I know it sounds trite, but it helps me sleep better at night."

She got it. She realized that what she'd seen tonight wasn't anything to Kenji. He wasn't worried because there had been times when his life had been in jeopardy and he'd been all alone. Her mind and her heart were shifting. This man who looked so calm and unflappable wasn't. She had to trust him to do his job. To keep himself safe as he had proved he could protect her.

"Like you said, we can talk when we get back," she told him. Because he was just becoming more attractive to her. Knowing the sacrifice he had made and was still making. He had a sense of justice that was just as strong as hers. His was a more physical kind, but she understood where he was coming from.

"I shouldn't have brought this up," she said, hoping she hadn't made things worse for him.

"You definitely should have. You matter to me, Daphne, I don't want you to ever be afraid for me. I'm not about to let anything happen to either one of us now that you are back in my life."

His words reassured her like nothing else could. They weren't out of danger, but they were together, and that was all she needed right now. She put her hand on his thigh as he continued to drive, and he put one on top of hers and squeezed.

It seemed to him as if the world was conspiring to keep him from being alone with Daphne. When they got back to Price Tower, Van was waiting and wanted a debrief on everything that had gone down.

"Lee has some information for you on the donor as well as a lead on Grey Joy," Van said, turning to Daphne. "We'll escort you there, and then I'll need to speak to Kenji alone, but Lee is fully trained as a bodyguard—"

"Mr. Price—"

"Van, please."

"Van, I feel safe here. You don't need to reassure me that I am," she said.

Van gave her that slow smile of his. "You are very safe here, but given how unpredictable the other places in your life have become, I thought you'd want to know. Nothing can get you when you're here."

"You're right," Daphne said. "Someone is expecting me to back down, and that's not my way."

"I could tell that from the moment we met," he said.

Kenji listened to his boss and the man who was like a brother to him talking to Daphne and being all calm and shit, but Kenji knew Van was anything but. His shoulders were tense, and he was smiling but it didn't make his eyes crinkle with their usual warmth.

What did Van know that Kenji didn't?

Van led the way to the elevator, and the three of them got on. There was silence as they went up, and Daphne adjusted her bag. "How's your shoulder?"

"Better," she said. "With everything else going on, the slight pain I have from that is hardly worth noticing."

"Indeed," Van said.

They got off on Lee's floor, where the other woman waited for them. "I've got good news for you."

"Great. I'm ready for some good news," Daphne said as she stepped off. She glanced back at him, and he just nodded at her. Not sure what she was trying to glean from him. Perhaps Daphne was waiting for him to make her feel like everything was cool.

She gave him a half smile as the elevator doors closed. Van hit the button for the penthouse…his own private living quarters.

"What's up?"

"I might need to pull you off Daphne," Van said.

"I'm not distracted or compromised," Kenji said.

"No, you're not. But I just got wind of…a connection from your past back in town."

"Who?" Kenji asked as they walked into Van's apartment. It was all modern art on the walls and furniture that Kenji thought of as modern Italian. The edges and angles that the Milan school favored.

There was only one person from his past that would concern Van enough to pull him off Daphne and into a private meeting.

"Kaitlyn Leo."

The Director.

Damn. There was only one reason why she wanted to meet, and it was to bring him back to The Farm and his old life. A life he'd been very clear he'd left behind.

"I am not leaving Daphne, but I can talk to Leo while Daphne is working tomorrow. Her office is secure now, and if she stays put with Xander guarding her, I think it could work." He would never say no to Van, but he wasn't leaving Daphne. Not until she was safe, and then he was going to figure out a way for them to try to be together. Their conversation in the car had clarified that for him.

But he needed to talk to her further and assure himself that she wanted him in her life too. She said she'd been scared, and he hated that for her. But he knew that leaving her again…it wasn't something he was willing to do.

"Kenji—"

"I'm not leaving Price," Kenji said. "This place is… You know I'm not one to talk about my feelings."

"You don't have to. The feeling is mutual. Do you want me to ask Leo to come here?"

Did he? The only benefit would be to Leo. She'd

check out Van's arrangement, and Kenji wasn't certain she wouldn't try to recruit Lee or Luna onto her team. She was smart and lethal and capable of making decisions that not everyone could. More than once she'd made a call that had civilian casualties in order to save many more. He had never really understood how she could do that, and that was why he'd eventually left the CIA.

"No. She'll just gather intel. I'm surprised she didn't just use her sources to get my cell."

"Professional courtesy," Van said.

"What were you before Price Security?" Kenji asked.

"That's a different life and has no bearing on what's happening now. Where do you want to meet?"

"Give me her number and I'll set it up. Thanks for not mentioning this in front of Daphne."

"No problem. Would it have meant anything to her?"

"She was in the same training program I was," Kenji said. "She'd know that if the Director wants to talk, it's not because she's in town and looking up a former colleague."

"Interesting. Let's go talk to Lee. She has found a lot of intel on the museum and the collection at the heart of Daphne's case."

Kenji followed his boss back down to Lee's office after Van had given him the Director's number, which he'd programmed into his phone. He was trying to dwell on why the Director had come to Los Angeles. She wasn't just in town. He wasn't sure if she had a mission for him or if it was something else.

When he walked into the room and saw Daphne, he realized that this meeting with the Director couldn't have come at a better time. There was no choice for him as there once had been between the adventure and excitement the CIA could give him compared a life with Daphne.

He wanted to try to make things work with her. No matter what it took. First, he had to eliminate whoever was threatening her life, and then he had to convince her that he wasn't a danger junkie.

Lee offered her a drink as they sat down at the conference table that had been moved into her office since the last time Daphne had been there. "I'm okay for now. What have you found?"

Lee smiled at her. "I'm going to project the info on the monitor over there so you can see it. No need to take notes. I'll send everything to you. Firstly, the archivist, Grey Joy. She's also a black market dealer of hard-to-find goods. I was able to set up a buy for tomorrow with her. She didn't have any of the items on your missing list, but when I asked around, she has been known to trade in some of the items currently on display in the museum," Lee said.

Daphne was trying to make this new information fit with what she knew of Grey. "Okay, which ones?"

"I've marked them in your file. I also found you someone who can authenticate them so you'll know they aren't replicas."

"Thank you. I've subpoenaed the museum's financial records, and I have to send some documents proving the relevance of this to the case. Can you give me the date when each of the items was sold?"

"I can. I'll add that to your file when we are done," Lee said.

Having a date range instead of just a general cry of "show me all your banking details" was what Daphne had been looking for to begin with, but there hadn't been a way to track the items. "How many items have gone from the black market back to the museum? Could the museum be the buyer?"

"Unlikely. The money seems to be coming from Ethiopia."

That didn't make sense. "Are you saying that someone in the country fighting to get the items returned is buying them and then selling them back to the museum?"

"I don't know that part. And I can't trace it further than a bank in Switzerland. I only got the details I did because I talked to one of the guys, and he let that slip and then shut me down. I don't think I'm going to be able to take that any further. But your client might have more information."

She might. Daphne made a note to call Marjorie as soon as she left Lee's office. This case was getting harder and harder to unravel. Each time she thought she'd won a battle in court and got what she asked for, it seemed to prove fruitless.

Cases were always complex and took time, but this one seemed like there was still so much to uncover. Each win she got led her to another mountain to climb.

"So, what time am I to meet Grey tomorrow?"

Kenji and his boss walked in as she'd asked that. She glanced over at Kenji, but his expression was unreadable. She remembered all they were trying to talk about in the car, and she still wanted to give them a chance to talk as a couple, but right now work was the priority.

"What about Grey?" Kenji asked as he sat down across from Daphne.

"I've set up a buy for tomorrow. I can get Rick to go. He's got four hours in the morning," Lee said.

"I'll do it," Kenji said. "Do you mind if Xander covers for me while you are at the office?"

Daphne definitely did. "I want to go with you."

"She won't talk if you're there."

"She saw you and knows we are working together," Daphne said. "What is this really about?"

As soon as those words left her mouth, she regretted it. "Never mind. Tell us what else you found, Lee. We can work out the details of tomorrow later."

Lee's fingers moved quickly over her keyboard, and the images on the monitor changed, but Daphne's attention was still on Kenji. What was going on? Why did he want to go alone? Was there some danger that she didn't know about?

"The original owner of the entire hoard that was donated to the Los Angeles Museum of Foreign Cultures was Jonathon Hazelton-Measham. The collection had been passed down to his son and then grandson, who sold it to the museum in 1985," Lee said. The amount she mentioned was a nice sum but nothing overly suspicious.

"In 2001, the grandson's son Henry contested the sale and said that his father was manipulated by the museum director, Franklin Lauder—the father of Pierce—into selling. They went to court, but the sale was legal."

"Was every item listed in the collection?" Daphne

asked, already texting her team to have them pull up the court documentation on the case.

"Yes, they were. There are seven items that are part of the case and don't show up anywhere on your inventory but were a part of the Arts of Africa exhibit that was shown in 2018. I've included that brochure in your file."

"Thank you," Daphne said. She had to stop thinking about Kenji. This was the kind of information she had needed to begin with. Now they had an original inventory, something that Lauder hadn't produced. "Were any of the items in the collection sold on the black market?"

"Two of them were, so possibly that's why they aren't in your inventory," Lee said.

Possibly, but Daphne would find out exactly what happened to them. "Is the grandson—what's his name?"

"Thomas Hazelton-Measham. He moved to Florida two years ago. I found an address, but it's a retirement park, and I couldn't find a phone number, but I did find an email. I put it in your file."

She appreciated how thorough Lee was. "This is great. I am going to be very busy tomorrow filing this with the court and getting everything in place. Thank you."

"No problem. It was fun doing this kind of project. Lately all I do is background checks and keep an eye on the crew," Lee said.

Daphne and Kenji went back to his apartment a few minutes later. Her mind was buzzing with all the new information she had to go through, but she wanted to talk to Kenji first.

Chapter 15

"Sorry for almost turning things personal in the meeting. I don't know what's going on with me tonight," Daphne said.

"You're being pushed to the edge, and it's stripping away the façade you use to keep everyone at bay. So you don't have time for anything that isn't real," he said. He'd seen it in clients before. There came a moment in every client where living with a bodyguard changed them. Even his wealthy clients who'd grown up with bodyguards around them developed their own way of dealing with it.

She shrugged and walked to the couch, dropping her bag and kicking off her shoes. "It feels like I'm living in someone else's life. What happened to my nicely ordered world?"

Kenji walked over to join her. His pants were torn from the fall he'd taken in the parking lot earlier that evening, and his jacket smelled like sweat. He shrugged out of it and toed off his shoes before sitting down next to her. "What can I do to help?"

She chewed her lower lip between her teeth. "I wish it were that easy. But you're a part of it too."

He got that. He was back in her life with no warning,

and the two of them were still attracted to each other, but he wasn't sure that was enough for her. He knew it wasn't. She'd told him in the car. That the danger of what he did scared her.

"Should we finish our conversation from the car?" he asked her.

"No. I realize now how silly that was. I like you, Kenji, and even if I never saw you again after my case goes to court, I'm not going to stop liking you or forget you," she said. "I was trying to draw a line in the sand and say I can only let myself have feelings for you if these criteria are met. But affection doesn't work that way."

No, it certainly didn't. It would have been easier for him if, after his clean break from Daphne all those years ago, he'd been able to keep her in the past. But he'd thought of her too often and more than once checked her out online. She'd been a sort of saving grace for him when he'd been deep in the shit in Afghanistan. Making decisions every day that cost lives and saved them. Trusting his gut had become harder and harder as everyone in that area had been so desperate.

"Not sure if this will help or not. But I used to google you after a bad day and just read about how successful you were, and it made me feel better…cleaner."

"Oh, Kenji," she said, leaning over and hugging him. He held himself stiff for a minute and then put his arms around her and drew her closer. The feel of her in his arms always shook him. He wasn't used to touching her, though he should have been.

She smelled of her floral perfume and *Daphne*, and there was so much comfort in the scent and the feel of her in his arms that he wasn't sure he would be able to let her go. He kissed the top of her head because sleeping with her now wasn't something he was sure was in his best interests.

The day had been a lot, and watching someone repeatedly stalking her bothered him. He didn't like that she had a stalker no one could identify. That there was no way to expose what was truly going on at the museum.

She sat back, tucking her legs under her body. "I'm glad I was able to help you."

Really, what else could she say to that? He hated that he was in his feelings and knew that he had to get that under wraps. "About tomorrow. It makes sense for me to talk to Grey. You made her nervous at the museum. I'll get the information."

Daphne tipped her head to the side, and her long black hair slid over her shoulder. "You don't honestly believe you aren't going to make her nervous. You look like a hit man or something lethal. That's not reassuring."

"It's supposed to be menacing. People take you seriously when you dress in a suit. And an all-black one makes them give me a wide berth. Which is what I need when I'm working."

"Only when you're working?" she asked.

"No. I use it when I travel too. Airports are the worst," he said.

"They are," she said. "Fine, you can talk to Grey by yourself. I really want to dig into all the information that Lee uncovered. She's a gem, by the way."

"She's the best," he agreed. "Do you think you can find a connection that will help you with your case?"

"She already has. Items that aren't marked missing

have disappeared from the inventory. Now I just have to take that list and see if they were sold. If they were, then we aren't any closer to finding out what the museum is trying to hide by ending the discussions with Marjorie and delaying this case," she said.

Kenji watched her as she talked about the case, once again struck by how beautiful she was when she was passionate about something. "Marjorie is lucky to have you on her side."

"The people of the Ethiopian Orthodox Church are. Lee also uncovered some black market sales where the buyers were in Ethiopia. So I'm going to have ask Marjorie some uncomfortable questions."

"Would she have hired you to cover her buys?" Kenji asked.

"I don't know. I don't think so, but after the last few days, I'm not really sure who I can trust anymore. My gut is telling me Marjorie isn't doing anything shady, but I thought my team would all come back clean."

She wrapped one arm around her waist and then looked over at him.

"You can trust me."

"I know."

"I have a lot of work to do tomorrow," she said. "I should go to bed."

"I need a shower." Kenji said, very aware that he wanted to keep her in his arms, but with the upcoming meeting with the Director on the horizon, he wasn't going to do anything else with Daphne.

Part of him wanted to discuss it with her, but she had a lot on her mind, and the information Lee had gathered was a lot to go through. He was here for her, not the other way around, he reminded himself.

His mom had taught him to rely on himself, always afraid that she'd die when he was young. It had always just been the two of them. No extended family at all to lean on. And his mom hadn't been someone who made friends easily. He saw that as an adult in a way that he hadn't has a child. He'd just enjoyed his Kenji and Mom time growing up.

He wished she was here to talk to now. She'd never had a chance to meet Daphne, but he thought his mom would say she was too smart for him and tell him he was lucky to have found her.

"Why are you looking at me that way?" she asked.

"How am I looking at you?" he countered.

"Like… I'm not entirely sure. A little bit like you're flirting with me, a little bit like you're happy, and a little bit like you have something to hide," she said.

"I'm a lot a bit of those things," he admitted.

"Flirting I get, and happy makes me feel a lot of joy. I'm going to assume it's because we are here together."

"You don't have to assume. I want to be here with you."

"I want you here too."

"Your life is in danger, and I am known for my skills at keeping people safe," he retorted.

"Humble brag?"

"That was a boast. Did I sound humble?"

She threw her head back and laughed. "No."

He couldn't help that he got hard when she laughed. It was just so nice to see her face relax and the stress and tension she carried with her all the time melt away. He wanted to see her that way more often.

"Good."

She tipped her head to the side as she twirled a strand of her hair around her finger. "That leaves whatever you are hiding."

Yeah, it did.

Was he going to tell her?

"In the car, when you said you didn't like the thought of me in danger, did you mean you were thinking of us a couple?"

She chewed her lower lip for a minute and stopped toying with her hair. "Yes."

Her voice was low and raw, some of the tension returning to her face. Which he hated.

"I have been too. The timing of this sucks because there is so much going on."

"It does. That doesn't mean I regret having you back in my life," she said. "I'm scared for you, and I'm not sure if, once my life goes back to its boring routine, you'll still be interested in me. Pretty much I work, come home and watch anime, and then go to bed to not sleep."

"I've always been interested, Daph. And I am now. Which anime?"

"Old ones. *Howl's Moving Castle* is my comfort watch. When I have a human rights case that is really tough to stomach, I just come home and lie on my couch eating potato chips and watching it. It's so sweet. It soothes me."

Kenji made a mental note of what she liked. He wanted to remember every detail so he could be what she needed from him.

"So, what are you hiding?" she asked again.

He rubbed the back of his neck. "The Director is in town and called Van to set up a meeting with me."

She seemed to sink back into herself as his words registered. Then she shook her head and straightened her spine, sitting taller next to him. "What does she want?"

"I'm not sure. Probably me to come back. The situation in the Ukraine is one that lends itself to my particular wheelhouse."

"How? What did you do for them, Kenji?" she asked.

"I worked with informants and set up strike teams to take down military targets," he said. There was no emotion in his voice because he'd had to shove all his feelings about every mission he'd completed in Afghanistan deep down and lock them away or he'd be sitting in a corner rocking and screaming.

"Are you considering it?" she asked. "Don't lie about this. I need to know the truth."

"I told you, you can trust me," he said. A little ticked she didn't.

"You did, but this…this is the CIA, and you've always loved it more than anything else. So I'm asking you, are you considering it?"

Kenji got where she was coming from and knew that her concerns were valid. He had always put the agency before anything else. It had been his dream to be a hero and to prove to his unknown father and to himself that he was worthy. But that dream had turned into a living nightmare during the war in the Middle East and the atrocities he'd witnessed and committed all in the name of justice and world peace. That dream had become something that Kenji couldn't face or be a part of anymore.

But how did he say that to Daphne without revealing the monster he'd become over there? The monster he still wasn't sure he'd caged. The man that he hoped he'd transformed into was in jeopardy. Kenji knew that more than anyone else.

"I'm not."

"It took you a long time to answer."

"It's complicated, but there is no place for the agency in my life now. I made that break because I knew that my future was somewhere else," he said.

There was more to his time at the agency than Kenji was ever going to share with her, which was totally his right. But he seemed a different man when he'd mentioned the Director, and the way he held himself now told her that he still had something unresolved with the CIA.

Not Daphne's problem.

Right, except it sort of was, because she was falling for him again. It didn't seem smart to continue to indulge her emotions and act like maybe they could have a life after this. No matter the discussion they'd just had. Kenji's life had been on a different path than hers since the moment he'd walked out her door all those years ago. She knew it, and she was pretty sure he did too.

That didn't make her want him any less. Was there a workaround where they could find a path they could walk together?

"Thanks for mentioning it to me," she said.

"I told you I'm not going back, and honestly, my life now isn't dangerous at all," he said.

As if the image of him being shot at and falling to the ground wasn't still etched clearly in her mind. "Try telling me that after you've changed out of your torn suit."

"Daphne."

Just her name. But there was so much emotion in that one word. Longing, she thought. That's what it was.

She longed for him too. Longed for a world where they could just be themselves, and people who took advantage of others didn't exist. Longed a place where they could just be together and the past would disappear.

But she'd never been a daydreamer. She was too practical for that. They'd either figure this out or they wouldn't. Either way, she'd continue living her life and doing her job. She wished she could be that pragmatic, but her heart was already flinching, trying to protect itself in case this didn't work out.

"The last thing I want is to return to that life," he said to her at last. "I…you might not know this about me, but I've always been a loner."

"Yeah, that I knew," she said. He'd stuck to himself during their training classes, and if they hadn't been paired together, she was pretty sure he wouldn't have spoken to her. They hadn't started dating until she left the program.

"Good. Then you'll understand this. Price Security isn't just a job to me. It's…like a family. I have people who I care about and who care about me, and it's not based on the results of my last mission."

He shoved his hand through his hair, and she realized how hard this was for Kenji to tell her. That made some of the tension deep inside of her dissipate.

"I'm glad you have them. But people cared about you before," she pointed out.

"Thanks. I think it's difficult to explain because your office…well, your boss hired us to protect you, and your team, including Alan, want to please you and make you happy. You are surrounded by something that I wasn't until Price."

She got it. One of the reasons she'd left the training program at The Farm was that she didn't want to go through life not really able to trust anyone. She wanted people in her office, even if they were simply being cordial, to act like her life mattered.

"I can tell by the comradery between you all that this is different," she said.

"It is. I can't go back to the man I was before or that life. Even if there was no you, I wouldn't. I can't refuse to meet with her, but I won't be accepting any assignments," Kenji said.

There was a finality to his voice that reassured her as nothing else could. She was happy to hear that resolve in his tone and hoped that it would be easy for him to decline whatever the director offered him. "Okay then. So, should we talk about tomorrow? I have a lot of information to add to the brief I've been working on and need to get it over to the courthouse."

Kenji seemed to relax as she changed the subject, which was good. She pulled her phone out and opened the notepad app so she could review the to-do list she'd already started. She lived by her lists.

"That'll keep you busy for how long?" he asked.

"Most of the morning. I'll send one of the assistants to file it in the afternoon. Hopefully either you'll be back with info on Grey Joy, or we'll have a number for Thomas Hazelton-Measham, and I can debrief him and get a statement," she said. Some of the fatigue she'd been feeling left her as she thought about all the work she needed to get done. It was nice to have something to sink her teeth into, and it felt like finally her case was taking shape.

She wanted to check in with a colleague in London who had worked on the British Museum case last year when thousands of artifacts had been stolen. Those items had made their way onto eBay, which she was going to assign her legal secretary to search tomorrow.

"I'll do my best. I'm going to try to talk to the director while I'm out as well. I don't want her to meet you," Kenji said.

"Why not?"

"You're smart and skilled, and she'll try to recruit you," he said succinctly. "And that's not something I can live with."

Daphne smiled when he said that. "She'd fail. I really love my work."

"Enough to take a bullet for it," he said wryly.

"Indeed," she said. She glanced down at the notepad. This night was made of all the things she liked about Kenji. Work, life and laughter all blending into one thing. It had been a long time since she'd laughed, which she hadn't realized until tonight when Kenji had been teasing her.

She was content with her life, but she was only now realizing how insular she'd made it.

Chapter 16

Kenji's suit was a dark gray today, and he had a floral-printed silk pocket square. His tie matched the suit, and his white shirt was pristine as always. She couldn't help the thrill that went through her as she looked at him. He'd styled his hair with some kind of product, because the fall of bangs that usually dominated his forehead was swept up and back.

He was quiet and contemplative, and given what they'd discussed the night before, she knew he had a lot on his mind.

She couldn't pretend she wasn't worried about him talking to the Director of the CIA. Kenji had said he wasn't interested in going back, but Daphne knew how hard it was to say no to the agency when they came knocking. She'd experienced it herself two years ago.

She'd been in The Hague working on a human rights case when she'd been approached. Even though she'd left the program before becoming an operative, the CIA still kept tabs on her and her movements, and they weren't afraid to ask for favors.

She'd declined because her client needed her full attention, but when the trail had ended, the operative sought her again. Once again, she'd declined, and that hadn't gone well.

How much worse would the pressure be on Kenji? She didn't want to imagine what he was dealing with. She wished she hadn't chickened out last night and had asked him to sleep with her.

She missed being in his arms, and that one quick hookup in the shower had whetted her appetite for him. She wanted more. Work had been the one thing she could count on to keep her distracted from the personal life she'd always wanted but never believed she'd find.

Now there was Kenji.

He'd denied that them having sex had been a reaction to the danger they'd both been in, but she wasn't entirely sure that was true. She was always confident, and had worn her favorite pantsuit today to reinforce that confidence in herself. But it was hard right now. Never had she felt this vulnerable.

She hated it.

"Are you okay?" he asked. There was concern in his tone and in his expression as he looked over at her.

"Yeah. Just…" She wasn't going to tell him she was nervous about his meeting with the Director. She'd never try to influence him in any way.

"It'll be okay," he said gruffly, then pulled her close, hugging her. She wrapped her arms around his body, resting her head on his shoulder. His spicy aftershave comforted her as much as his arms did.

What was she going to do if he left when this case was over? Because no matter how she chose to frame it, she still wanted him in her life. For the first time since she'd given up trying to make her mom love her, she wanted to figure out what she could do to make Kenji love her.

That wasn't a road she wanted to be on, but there she was. She had no way of changing it either. The case was a distraction, but in her heart, she knew that she wanted him to be safe and care about her and stay in her life.

Van waited for her in the garage. He smiled as he led her to a Dodge Charger. Having been in the garage before, she knew they had a fleet of them and two big black Hummer limos. Kenji had been dressed as always in a suit. Today it was gray with a white shirt and thin dark gray tie. She'd wanted to say something to him before he went to meet the Director, but she hadn't found the right thought, so had just waved goodbye to him.

She wanted to move on the brief she was writing and get the request for financial records in at the courthouse today. She'd messaged her team to get in early if they could. Most of them would be, but Janice, a paralegal, had to take her kids to school first. Which was perfectly fine.

Daphne's own mom had acted like Daphne was a stumbling block to her successful career and had often driven like a maniac through traffic and dropped Daphne off before the teachers got to school so she could get into her office early. Her father was an ER surgeon, so he wasn't always available to take her to school.

She shook her head and brought herself back to the present. Who cared? It was in the past, but it was Christmastime, and that always stirred up longings for a childhood that she'd never had and was never going to. Normally she just worked through it and didn't let it bother her.

Having Kenji back in her life was calling up her emotions and making her think of things she'd assumed she'd resolved years ago.

"I'll stay out of your way this morning," Xander said as they got to her office.

"Kenji usually just stands by the door and glares at everyone, but I don't mind if you use one of the guest chairs. My staff and I will probably spend most of our time in the conference room down the hall once they are all in," she said.

"I'm good here," Van said, leaning against the wall. "I'll try not to glare."

"Thanks. That'll be a change for my team," she said.

She went behind her desk and started to go through her emails. One response to the email she'd sent last night before going to bed was from her friend in London. She flagged it and continued to move through the messages.

There was one from Pierce Lauder, apologizing for the attack on her at the museum and telling her that the deputy director should have been with her. He said he'd be back at the museum on Saturday if she wanted to come and look at the collection again.

She flagged that one as well.

Alan walked into her office carrying three to-go coffee cups. He started to hand one to Van, then did a double take. "Sorry. I thought you'd be Kenji. Want a double espresso?"

"No thanks. I take mine with lots of milk and sugar," Van said.

Alan nodded and walked to her desk, handing her a chai latte. "Morning, Boss. I started running through the shared task list this morning. I took the financial brief since I was already working on it. Having the specific date of the one sale will give me a good starting range."

She took the chai from him, smiling. "I thought you might want that one. We can work in the conference room today. I'm going to ask Janice to do the eBay search."

Alan nodded. "I'll let the rest of the team know to meet in the conference room and that you have a new bodyguard."

"Just for this morning," Daphne said. "This is Van Price. Van, this is Alan."

The two men nodded before Alan left her office. She cleared the rest of her emails and then opened the one from her friend.

Several thousand items from the British Museum's collection had been stolen or marked missing or damaged, and it was revealed that a staff worker had been facilitating the theft but hadn't been charged in the burglary. Her friend had sent her some information on his case. He'd represented the whistleblower who had purchased an item off eBay and then realized it was the property of the British Museum.

Interesting. Other than the burlap bag that the censer had been in, she wasn't sure if the items from the Los Angeles Museum of Foreign Cultures were labeled in any way. She hadn't noticed anything as obvious as a tracking number on the censer, but she hadn't really examined it either.

She and her staff spent the morning writing the brief that Alan would take to the court that afternoon. The financial documents request, and now that they had proof of a sale of an item, Daphne felt confident they would be granted something. The other was a detailed request for the discrepancies between the donated items and the current inventory.

Pierce had told them the inventory that he'd provided had all of the items, but now that Lee had pulled the complete donation paperwork, there were differences that needed to be explained.

Van stood quietly in the corner, not glaring as he'd promised, but he was on guard. Daphne couldn't help noticing the differences between him and Kenji. Both of them gave off an aura of, well, *menace* wasn't the right word, but they were definitely not men that any-one would mess with…but they also made her feel safe.

Her staff worked on. They decided to order lunch, which she put on her company card. Finally it seemed like this case was coming together, and Daphne had a call scheduled with Marjorie for later that afternoon in which she'd update her and hopefully ask her to look into bank records in her country. As the cultural min-ister, maybe she'd have some pull. Daphne certainly hoped so.

Sitting in the Charger next to the park near the Los Angeles Museum of Foreign Cultures, Kenji was on guard. The Director was due to arrive any moment, which he could attribute his edginess to, but it was more than that. There was something building inside him that felt dangerous.

It was tied to Daphne. Talking to her last night had been unexpected and had made him realize how much he wanted things to work out with her. Not just to work out. He needed them to find a way to be together, and keeping her safe was his top priority.

He wanted to question Grey Joy. A part of him knew he'd use whatever methods necessary to get her to talk even if it would be beyond his scope. This was a civil mission, not a CIA one, so those methods weren't acceptable. He knew that, but his gut wasn't hearing him. That made him dangerous to everyone, including Daphne.

It was some kind of screwed-up hamster wheel he was on. Needing to be lethal to protect her, but being lethal would make him into that monster he'd been before he'd retired, and then the monster would put her in danger. Then back to trying to protect her.

He shoved his sunglasses up on his head and rubbed his thumb and forefinger over his eyes. He had a headache from trying to figure this out.

A smart man would ask to be replaced. But Kenji wasn't going to do that. No matter how capable the other members of Price Security were, he had to be the one to watch over Daphne and keep her safe.

He heard a rap on his door. Turning carefully, he saw her standing there. Perfectly coiffed hair and form-fitting black suit.

The Director. He hit the unlock button and gestured for her to get into the car. He had already decided he was going to be in control of this meeting. Or at least pretend he was. He knew that the Director had been in his head since Van had mentioned her name.

She was a tall woman at five foot eight inches and had blond hair she always wore pulled back in a low ponytail. She favored navy suits, and today's version had a gray pinstripe in it. She had on a cream-colored silk shirt underneath and wore a pair of dark aviator-style Ray-Bans. When she got into the car, there was no scent of perfume, just a hint of the cool air from this December Los Angeles day.

She closed the door behind her and turned to look at him.

"Thank you for taking this meeting."

Be cordial he warned himself. "As if I had an option."

Yeah, he wasn't in the mood to play the game today. He wanted her taken care of so he could find Grey Joy and move closer to finding out who had shot at Daphne and was now stalking her.

She gave him a savvy smile. Every nerve in his body tingled, and he felt himself shifting into operative mode. It took a moment for him to pull back and remind himself he was out of that life.

"I've missed your honesty, Wada," she said.

She always referred to him and all of her operatives by their last names.

"Why are we here?" he asked.

"I need you. There's a *delicate* mission that you are perfect for," she said.

He pulled his sunglasses back down as he turned his head so they weren't making eye contact. He was skilled, all right, but not the only one who had his training or his success in missions. "You need a retired agent?"

"I do. Interested?" she asked in that low, modulated tone he knew she used when she was probing. She wanted something from him.

"No." One-word answers were the only way to communicate with her. *Keep it quick and simple and get out of here.*

"Wada, I wouldn't be here if I thought you couldn't handle this."

Flattery. She was stroking him, hoping that it would get him to ask for more. He wished it wasn't working.

He swiveled his head to face her. "I know I can handle it. I just don't want to. I'm happy with my current assignment."

"Protecting a lawyer. You were made for so much more than that."

She'd overplayed her hand, Kenji thought. He wasn't going to agree to anything now that she was insulting the peace he'd found working as a bodyguard. As if this role wasn't as important as the one he'd held at the agency.

"Maybe. But it suits me. I like that I have a life here. I'm not the same man I was before I retired," he told her.

"You've never said no when your country needed you," she said.

"Going for the jugular? If sentiment won't sway, try patriotism." Sure, he wanted to defend his country. The family he'd made for himself all were citizens of it. But he also wasn't blindly going to rush out to destabilize a government or turn someone's wife against them without knowing what was at stake.

She gave him that half smile again. "It was worth a try."

It was definitely worth a try. He hated to say no, but he knew that there was almost always a list of people she would ask. "I'm sure you'll find someone who will say yes."

"I will. But I want you for this," she said.

Oh, no. Now he was curious. Why him? Should he

ask about the details? Fuck no. He wasn't going back. He'd already decided that.

He just shrugged. There was no way he was going to let her get out of the car without telling him the mission. He hated that there was still that part of him drawn to the intrigue the Director always brought with her.

"Don't you want to at least hear the mission parameters before deciding?"

"Sure."

Internally he punched the brick wall that he mentally kept in place for dealing with his frustration. At this moment, he had everything he had been craving for the last few years. His found family, and now Daphne was back in his life.

But one little piece of bait from the Director and he was eyeing it, trying to see if he could get it off the hook and keep his freedom.

He knew the answer to that.

It was no.

There were no half measures with the agency or with her. She wasn't going to give him one little mission for the thrill of it and then let him retire again.

Kenji honestly wasn't sure he'd be able to go back to the old life and then return to Price Security and be content. For him, it was one or the other. The man he'd been on his way to becoming before he'd retired was still there.

The man who was half monster. The man who'd said goodbye to his humanity to achieve results at any cost. That man wasn't one who could hold Daphne in his arms.

Kenji knew it. He also knew his answer had to be no.

"I thought you might. It involves an international illegal art and antiquities operation in LA—"

Was this tied to Daphne's case? He couldn't help but feel that it might be. Not that he was going to let Kaitlyn drag him back into working for her. "Let me stop you there. My days of using local informants are done. The answer is still no."

She took her sunglasses off. "What if the informant I have is your friend's husband, Nicholas DeVere?"

WTF? What was Nick involved in? The billionaire was known for dealing in favors, using his wealth to help out others in order to cultivate relationships.

"I'll speak to him. But you're not using him. I'll pass the information to you, and then you leave him out of it," Kenji said. "I mean it, Kaitlyn. Do you understand me?"

"He came to us."

Kenji didn't give a crap about that. He wasn't letting the Director use Luna's husband. "He doesn't know what you will do to him. He's finally safe after a lifetime of being stalked. You take care of the threat and get it away from him."

"I could if I had my best agent back working for me," she said.

This wasn't something he could just say no to. He needed to talk to Nick, and damn that he was still trying to help Daphne and keep her safe.

"I'm in town for a few more days at a conference. Call me and let me know your answer," she said, getting out of the car and walking away.

Kenji grabbed the steering wheel hard with both hands, wanting to punch something. She'd just made him an offer he couldn't refuse. This might be a lead that could help him find out who was behind the attacks on Daphne. Plus the fact that Nick and Luna were family, and he couldn't allow them to be in danger any more than he could allow Daphne to.

Chapter 17

The morning was intense in the conference room. Everyone on her team was focused on the new briefs they were writing to make sure that everything was in place. Janice had started searching eBay for the items in the inventory, while Alan worked on the financials.

Janice came in in a rush. "Sorry I'm late."

Janice had long blond hair that she habitually wore in a messy bun. Her clothes were clean but older or from the secondhand shop, as most of the money she made went to supporting her family. She'd told Daphne that she and her husband had decided it was worth the sacrifice to send their kids to a private school, so all of the money they both made went toward that.

She worked hard as a paralegal. Daphne was mentoring her and had arranged for a scholarship for Janice to an online school so she could continue her education and keep working. She was one semester away from attaining her law degree and then would sit for the bar exam.

"I've forwarded you an article about the British Museum controversy where items stolen from the museum ended up on eBay. Could you start a search and try to match it against any of the items on our list?"

"Yeah, no problem," Janice said.

"How was the school run?"

"Not bad at all. Abby got all the words on her spelling list, and Umberto sang his solo for me three times," Janice said with a smile.

Daphne often wondered if she'd feel the same way about her children if she risked having them. Or were her maternal instincts the same as her own mother's? Nonexistent. She shook her head. She really didn't want to go down that road. "Sounds like a good morning."

"It has been. I'll get on this right away."

Janice moved to the end of the conference table, took her seat and started working on her laptop. Daphne noticed Van observed everyone in the room and kept his attention moving from person to person.

She felt safe with him, but she missed Kenji's presence. Which wasn't the smartest thing for her to be thinking since he had a meeting with the Director today.

Cass, who'd been on Daphne's team the longest, was back from vacation. When she entered, Daphne signaled her to come to the end of the table so they could work together.

Cass was a willowy blonde, and as soon as they'd spotted each other in the break room, they'd both smiled and become instant friends. That hadn't really happened often with Daphne, and she treasured the bond with Cass.

It was as if they'd known each other all their lives, and there was nothing that Daphne didn't feel comfortable telling the other woman. Cass had been married when they met, so as long as she'd known her, she'd known Gerry. He was easygoing and tended to show up unannounced when they were working late with dinner for the three of them.

The two were like family to Daphne, so the last thing she was going to allow was the trouble dogging her with this case to spill over onto either of them. Or any of her staff, for that matter. She needed to know they were safe.

But sometimes when digging through information, things were revealed that could be dangerous. Daphne always thought it was so interesting the facts that people tried to hide.

Cass laughed at something Janice said as she stopped to talk to the other woman before making her way down the room. Everyone liked Cass. Alan had a crush on her, and Daphne noticed that even Van seemed to turn toward her more often. She was just one of those women who made everyone feel good, so they liked to be around her.

Daphne tried to be that way, but it wasn't always easy. It was hard to fight the memory of being told to leave the room when her mother entered. Or told to not speak. It made her want to be invisible, and her entire adult life after her breakup with Kenji, she'd been forcing herself to be visible.

But sometimes she preferred the shadows, where she could observe and sort through the facts and precedents and figure out a way to win the case.

"I freaked when I heard you were shot, but Gerry insisted you would have texted if you needed me," Cass said when they took a break to stretch their backs and walked to the corner of the room where there were no windows per Van's instructions.

"Yes. I'm sure Gerry would have ordered a hit on me if I interrupted your first real vacation in five years."

"He wouldn't because he'd be afraid of having to investigate himself, but otherwise you're right," Cass said with a laugh. "You haven't said how you are."

"I'm...okay."

"Girl, that doesn't sound convincing."

"I know. It's the best I can do. The other bodyguard... he's the one from my past that I mentioned."

"The total d-bag who dumped you without a reason and walked away?" Cass said.

Hearing her relationship with Kenji summed up like that made her cringe. But late-night drinks with girlfriends were for spilling all the emotional vitriol that was stuck inside.

"He's not a total d-bag. In fact, I'm starting to fall for him again."

Cass put her hand on Daphne's elbow and turned them so their backs were to the room. "For real? Or like Whitney Houston falling for Kevin Costner in *The Bodyguard* and him leaving her at the end?"

"For real," she said. "I was planning to ignore him and the past, but you know how I am."

"You need answers. That's why you're such a good lawyer."

"I know, and so crap at relationships."

"Not all of them. We've been friends for twelve years now."

"We have, but you're a lot like me."

"Totally awesome and kickass is how everyone should be," Cass said.

Daphne hugged her friend. Usually in the office she kept things professional. "I missed you."

"Missed you too. Gerry confiscated my cell as soon as we got to the mountain retreat."

Which made sense given that Cass was a workaholic like her. "Did you have fun?"

"You know what, I did," Cass said. "We hiked and cooked together. And neither of us were called to work. It was nice."

It sounded idyllic. What would it be like if she and Kenji were alone for a week? No phones or threats? She wanted that, she thought. Maybe… She still didn't know what would happen when the case was over.

"Hey, Daphne, we are thinking of ordering in from Burger Boy. You two want something?" Alan asked.

They both turned to face the room.

"Girls night soon," Cass said before looking at Alan. "You know I want a Reuben extra kraut."

"Gross," Daphne said.

Cass just stuck her tongue out at Daphne.

"Italian on rye for me. Thanks," Daphne said.

Alan finished compiling the order. Pam ran out to take a call from her husband as Alan placed it. Van had declined food, saying he'd eat when Kenji got back.

She almost asked if he was on his way but stopped herself, instead turning back to the brief. She'd found a piece from the list of donated items Lee had provided that now belonged to a private collector and was on display in their nightclub, Madness. The name was just N. DeVere.

The billionaire?

She'd never been to Madness but had heard it was unique. The item that N. DeVere had purchased was a shield made for one of their emperors. The hide shield had a pendant made from a lion's mane on the front. The inner shield and handle were covered with red saffron leather while the upper side cover was blue silk studded with bands of silver and other silver gilt. It was a remarkable item and part of the regalia that had made up the Maqdala collection. The shield was now on permanent display behind the bar.

"Alan, can you add this to the financial brief 2015? We need to know when the shield was sold and purchased by N. DeVere."

"DeVere?" Van asked.

"Yes, do you know him?"

"Very well. You think he's connected to this?" Van asked.

"He purchased an item from an online auction, according to the Madness website, but I'll have to talk to him to confirm it," Daphne said.

"I can arrange that," Van offered.

"The sooner I can speak to him the better," Daphne said. She wanted to have some facts from DeVere before she filed this brief.

Van tapped his ear, and Daphne realized he had an earpiece in. "Contact Luna. I need to speak to Nick regarding…"

Van glanced over at Daphne.

"The Tewodros Shield purchased in 2015 for Madness."

Van relayed the information back to Lee and then resumed standing in the corner. Daphne imagined she'd hear from Van or Lee when they had the information.

"Where did you find these guys?" Cass asked under

her breath. "I didn't realize they worked for Nicholas DeVere."

"Carl hired them."

"He must have been scared when you were shot," Cass said, her fingers moving over the keyboard as she ran a search on Price Security. But the website was just their name and the tagline *Security is priceless, and your life is worth the price.*

"How did Carl know about them?" Cass asked.

"He's got connections," Daphne said. "Back to the brief. Pull as much information on the piece as you can. I want to demonstrate that this piece was a key part of the collection and just disappeared. It's on Marjorie's list, and the museum has ignored that it's gone."

"On it."

Daphne had a response from Marjorie, who said she'd talk to the finance minister and see what information she could find. They arranged to have a chat later the next day, and Daphne hoped to be able to tell her about the piece that DeVere now owned. Which would add another complication to her case.

If pieces were in the hands of private collectors, that would make it more complicated. The auction houses were within their rights to list and sell pieces that came from museum collections, and in 2015, the public hadn't been aware that contested items made up the backbone of several museums' collections. This was getting messier and messier.

Kenji moved his car around to the employee parking lot to wait for Grey Joy, and his move paid off. He noted that she arrived in a yellow beater of a Ford. She parked the car and then got out, slinging a big canvas messenger bag over her shoulder. She walked into the museum, and Kenji waited to see who else entered. A few minutes later, the deputy director who he'd met yesterday arrived, along with a few more museum staff.

He hadn't thought about doing a stakeout to watch the museum, but now that he was here, it made sense. He tapped his earpiece and waited for Lee to get back to him.

"Sorry for the delay. Busy morning. What's up?"

"Do we have anyone who could watch the museum back entrance just to track movement? Or could we tap into a security feed?" Kenji asked. "There are a lot of people in and out, and I can't identify them all."

"Let me see what I can do," Lee said. He heard her fingers moving over the keyboard in the background. "They have a security camera set up for the back entrance and the main parts of the museum. Seems like the cameras on the archives and file rooms...aren't working. Hmm...let me see if I can find out who monitors them, and maybe we can make a call and get them fixed. Any areas you want me to watch?"

"All of them," he said dryly. "I'm not sure who is responsible for coming after Daphne, but it's definitely tied to the pieces that are missing. And all of these guys are still suspects."

"All right, I'm on it. Also, just to keep you up to date, Nick has one of the pieces that disappeared from the museum."

Kenji wasn't too pleased to hear Nick's name again. "Why? How?"

"He bought it at auction in 2015. Daphne is trying to get more information, and Luna's gone to help out."

"Thanks for keeping me in the loop," Kenji said. "Can you track a yellow Ford?"

He rattled off the license plate number, and Lee agreed to use an algorithm to track the car's movements through speed cameras and ATMs throughout the city.

"Let Van know I'll go and talk to Nick before heading back to Daphne's office," Kenji said. Now that he had a connection to Daphne's case, Kenji felt fairly certain that he could do that without raising suspicion.

He hated that one discussion with the Director and he was back to keeping secrets. But he wanted to get to the bottom of this. He suspected she'd come to him because the CIA had no purview to operate inside the borders of the United States. So she couldn't work Nick as an informant.

"Will do. When should I tell him to expect you?"

Forty minutes if the traffic was good to get to Nick and maybe twenty minutes to talk to him. "A couple of hours."

"Yeah, traffic is a bitch today. I'll keep you posted with the security company and footage if I can get it. Might need to ask for a tap. I'll contact Detective Miller and see if we can work with the art squad."

"Thanks. Let's keep this between us until we have something. Daphne's got enough to worry about now," Kenji said.

"No problem. Later."

Kenji tapped the earpiece to mute it and then headed toward downtown, where Nicholas DeVere lived and worked in an Art Deco–style building. He'd converted two floors into a nightclub called Madness. A year ago he'd hired Price Security when his lookalike bodyguard had been murdered in his place. So Kenji knew the building pretty well.

A lot of the passive security measures they'd put in place were still there. Including access to the parking garage by Price Security. He parked the car and headed up to Nick's office. Not surprised to find Luna waiting for him at the elevator.

"Lee told me you were on your way. I've already relayed the information about the museum piece to Daphne," Luna said. "But it's always nice to see you."

"I'm glad to hear that. I'm actually here for something else as well," Kenji said.

Luna was like a sister to him, and they were close enough that he didn't want her to be surprised by whatever Nick was involved in. Not that Kenji suspected the other man was doing anything illegal. But Nick thought he was unbreakable and wouldn't worry about danger to himself.

Luna sighed. "What else?"

"I'm not sure, but I need to talk to Nick. My old boss at the CIA asked me to cultivate a local informant who has some information regarding an international art and antiquities smuggling operation."

"And Nick's the informant?"

He nodded. He could tell by her face that it was news to her. "Let's go and see him, shall we?"

Kenji almost felt sorry for Nick, but knew the other man would be able to soothe Luna. He got where Luna was coming from all too well. It was sort of how he'd felt when he realized that Daphne had put herself in danger by going out in the alleyway that first night by herself.

It staggered him as he realized that he'd already been falling back in love with her then. Maybe he'd never fallen out of love with her. And that was why everything felt so intense for him.

Nicholas DeVere smiled at Kenji as they walked into his office. His assistant, Finn Walsh, was at his side. "Hello, Kenji. Long time."

"Good to see you, Finn," he said to the other man.

"Are you here about the piece I purchased?" Nick asked. "Finn is pulling the paperwork as we speak."

"I'm here about something else. My old boss got in touch wanting me to liaise with an informant with a connection to an illegal smuggling ring," Kenji said.

"Hell."

Nick shook his head and immediately turned to face Luna. "I didn't want you to find out."

But Nick wasn't speaking to Kenji. Instead, he spoke to his wife.

"Well, I did. You're not supposed to keep things from me. We can discuss it later. Kenji, what does she want?" Luna asked.

"She wants to use your connection and you," Kenji said. "She needs an in with the smugglers."

"What I got was an offer to attend a private auction. I'm not sure that anyone else can go but me."

"I could," Finn said.

"No," Nick and Kenji both said at once.

"Why not?"

"It's dangerous," Nick said. "You're too valuable, Finn."

"Once the Director has your name, she'll never forget it," Kenji added.

"Would you be willing to RSVP to the event and share the information with me? I'll relay the information to the Director."

"Sure. Will that be enough?"

"It'll have to be. She can stake it out or send her own undercover agent in."

"Or I could go," Finn said.

He walked over to Finn and put his hand on the other man's shoulder, because Finn looked as if he were still considering offering himself to help out. "No matter how enticing she makes the work sound, only say yes if you're willing to give up the life you have here. There's no way to live in both worlds."

Finn's mouth got tight, and he nodded.

"Time for me to head back to Daphne."

"I'll see you out," Luna said.

They had just stepped off the elevator when he got an emergency call to report to Daphne's office.

"Go," Luna said. "I'll talk to Nick and Finn and keep them both safe. Are you going back to the CIA?"

"No," Kenji said.

"I'm glad. I've got this. Go now," Luna said, hugging him as he left her.

He tapped his earpiece. "What's going on?"

"Poison. EMTs are on their way. Van wants backup to question and search the area."

"Daphne."

"Fuck, sorry. She wasn't poisoned. One of her team members…but it was her drink that had the poison in it."

Chapter 18

Daphne freaked out when Cass stopped talking mid-sentence and collapsed next her. Van noticed it and was immediately on his earpiece, calling for the ambulance.

"Does anyone have first aid training?" Van asked.

"I do," Janice said.

Janice rushed over to them. Cass was convulsing, and Daphne held her friend's head so it didn't hit the table. "Clear the table and let's lay her on it."

Everyone worked together to get Cass up on the table. Janice took her pulse and checked for blocked airways. "Does she have any conditions?"

"No. She's usually very healthy. What is going on?" Daphne asked.

The EMTs rushed in and started working on Cass. After asking what had happened before she collapsed, an expert was called and they tested her drink and found it had been contaminated with strychnine.

"What? Someone poisoned her?" Daphne was scared when she heard that. Everyone looked white as a ghost.

"No one leaves this room," Van said as soon as the EMTs took Cass out on a stretcher. "The cops are on their way."

"I don't think anyone in here would hurt Cass," Daphne said. She looked around at her staff. They'd had such a productive and fun morning doing work they all loved and were passionate about.

Alan glanced at the cup that Cass had been drinking from and put his hand on his throat. "I think Cass got your drink, Daphne."

She looked at the table and realized her friend had. The cup was clearly marked with her name and her order. Daphne felt lightheaded and sank to her own chair. Cass and she always shared a drink because the shakes were too decadent for one person. Her hand was shaking as she started to reach for it.

Van stopped her, catching her hand. He stood between her and the rest of the room.

"Alan, you brought the order up, correct?"

"Yes."

"Please sit here so I can watch you. Everyone else can sit at the other end of the table. No texting while we wait for the cops, and no talking."

"Van, this isn't necessary," Daphne said, but she was having a hard time controlling the trembling inside her body. She felt weird like she was about to collapse, which was just her nervous system reacting to what was going on. She knew that. There wasn't anything wrong with her. It was Cass…

"I have to text Gerry and tell him to meet Cass at the hospital," she told Van.

He moved so he could look at her while keeping the entire room in his view. "Who?"

"Her husband. I'm not asking you. I'm just keeping you in the loop," Daphne said. Now that her initial scare was passing, she was getting mad and needed to take some control.

She texted Gerry and gave him the bare bones she knew. Told him she'd stop by the hospital after the cops cleared her to leave the office. Then put her phone back on the table.

"Why is Alan separated?"

"He's the one who brought the food up," Van said in the low rumble of a voice that made her aware he was a dangerous man. The smile he usually had on around her had made her almost forget it. "We need to make sure he's not the poisoner."

"I didn't poison anyone."

"Well, someone did," Van said. "You also suggested the restaurant."

"We always get lunch from there," Janice said. "No one knows the people who work there."

Pam nodded along while looking at Alan, who had gotten more sullen and quiet as time passed. Daphne wasn't sure she blamed him. He'd already answered questions about his connection to Pierce Lauder, yet she wasn't sure that he wasn't working with his uncle. But poisoning her?

He noticed her looking at him and then shook his head. "I've already given you my word that I'm not working with my uncle. Do you really think that I would be complicit in something that would harm you? And if I was, do you think I'm so incompetent that I would put it into a drink I know you and Cass share?"

He had a point. Everyone in this room knew that she and Cass shared the shake. The delivery person or the one who prepared her order wouldn't. "Did you see the delivery guy?"

"Yeah. He had on a Burger Boy uniform and baseball cap," Alan said.

Van watched the play between all of them. He tapped his earpiece as he'd done a few times while the EMTs had been in the building and asked Lee to send Luna to Burger Boy and dispatch Xander and Rick to search for the delivery driver.

Detective Miller arrived a few minutes later, along with two cops and Xander, who informed Van that the building was locked down, but Daphne was afraid it was probably too late to save her friend. The poison was odorless, and it was only Cass's collapse that had brought their attention to it.

"Burger Boy reported their driver as missing," Detective Miller said. "I've put out an APB for his vehicle. We're going to need to take everyone's statement."

"Not a problem," Alan said loudly. "I'll be happy to tell you what I know."

Daphne felt bad that Alan was the target of so much suspicion. But Cass was in the hospital. Gerry had arrived and texted that they had pumped her stomach and were keeping her for observation, but she should be able to go home later that night.

"Cass is going to be okay," Daphne told the team.

"I'm glad to hear that," Alan said.

"Me too," Janice and Pam said.

Individually they were all questioned by the detective, and she called in a forensic team to dust the take-out bags and cups for prints. Daphne kept watching the door, waiting for Kenji, but he didn't arrive.

* * *

Kenji rushed back to the Mitchell and Partners office building. Traffic was heavy, but he used all of his evasive driving skills and a lot of speed and intimidation to get to Wilshire Boulevard. He knew that Daphne hadn't been poisoned, but the fact that someone on her staff had been was worrying.

Whoever was threatening Daphne was stepping up their attacks. He almost wondered if they should pretend she had been poisoned to shake them out, but he heard via his earpiece that the cops had already been there and reported that a woman named Cass Smith had been the victim.

It was strychnine, which was odorless, so the fact that the woman had collapsed was the only way they had been able to identify it. Kenji pulled into a parking space just as Rick walked out of the building.

"What's going on?" Kenji asked.

"The restaurant reported that their driver hasn't reported back to work. Detective Miller put out an APB on the car. I'm going to check the parking lot to see if I can find him."

Rick caught him up on all the details and then turned to check out the parking lot for the driver. There was a chance he might have been knocked unconscious or worse.

"Want some help?" Kenji asked.

He knew that Van was keeping Daphne safe, and Kenji needed a few moments to get himself under control. To figure out how to be cool when he saw Daphne. But he wasn't going to be cool. He couldn't be. Not with her.

He was still agitated from his meeting with the Director, where she'd in essence threatened his family, and now his woman had almost been poisoned. Kenji was on edge in a way that he hadn't been since…well, since Afghanistan. He didn't like the emotions that rolled around inside of him, and he was certain he couldn't control them.

"Yeah. Left?"

Kenji nodded and started sweeping to the left of the parking lot. He tapped his earpiece to unmute it as he walked, looking for any signs. "Do we know how anyone would have been sure the food was meant for Daphne?"

"She used her credit card to pay for it," Van said. "Lee, can someone monitor her cards?"

"They could, but it's a better bet that someone inside is a mole."

"Yeah, Detective Miller is going hard on Field," Van said.

The one connected to the museum director. "Anyone else acting odd?"

"The legal secretary keeps crying," Van said. "I think she's scared, and rightly so."

"Pam Beale?"

"Yes, why?"

"She said something odd when I took her picture and almost broke down," Kenji said. "Lee?"

"On it. I'll dig around and see if there's something we missed," Lee said.

Kenji kept walking and noticed one of the hedges along the side of the building had been crumpled like by a foot or something. He moved closer and noticed a man's leg. A guy in jeans and a Burger Boy T-shirt was collapsed on the ground. Kenji knelt to check his pulse, which was low but there.

He unmuted his earpiece. "Found the driver. Southeast corner of the building. Unconscious. Low pulse."

"I'll call for an ambulance," Lee said.

"I've alerted Miller, and Officer Jones is on his way down. Rick?" Van asked.

"On my way, Boss," Rick answered.

Kenji glanced up as his coworker jogged over to his location. There was blood oozing from a wound at the back of the delivery man's neck as well as what looked like a Taser wound on his chest. The burn marks were left on the T-shirt.

"This guy's going to have one hell of headache," Rick said dryly.

"He's lucky that's all he's going to have," Kenji said.

Rick snorted. Kenji glanced up and saw a hint of a smile on Rick's face. "This is turning into something bigger."

"I agree, but what? I can see wanting her out of the picture, but Mitchell will just assign another lawyer to the case," Kenji said.

"Maybe they have a lawyer they want to replace her," Rick said. "Makes sense with all the attacks."

"Yeah, but first they wanted the censer she found," Kenji said.

"Cop incoming," Rick said, walking over to greet the officer as Kenji stood up and turned to do the same.

"We'll take it from here," the officer said. Kenji and Rick walked back toward the main entrance.

"God, I wish I still smoked," Rick said.

Kenji just clapped his friend on the shoulder and offered him a pack of gum. Rick took it, unwrapped two pieces and shoved them into his mouth. "Thanks."

"Rick, head over to Topanga. The APB came back, and the driver's car was abandoned. Miller is sending some beat cops, but maybe you can talk to the locals and get a description of the driver," Van said.

"On it, Boss," Rick said, giving Kenji a little salute before he walked toward his car.

Kenji continued into the building. The two large Christmas trees that flanked the reception desk looked out of place and too damned cheery given that a woman had been poisoned.

But Kenji knew better than most that the holiday season didn't mean everyone was going to play nice. Crime still happened, and criminals like the one who was after Daphne weren't going to take a few weeks off.

This latest attack was like Rick and he had discussed: designed to take Daphne out of the picture. Perhaps now that the museum had learned the censer had been returned, they worried what else Daphne would find out.

Was she closer to uncovering what was really going on than either of them realized?

He wasn't too sure. But he was going to keep her by his side from now on. He had a good lead on Grey Joy, and Kenji wasn't above using whatever means necessary to get information from her.

If she was the one who'd called Daphne to the alleyway, she probably knew who the mole was at Mitchell and Partners and who was threatening Daphne.

Xander snagged him as he walked to the elevator. "Hey, got a minute? You're better with security footage than I am."

"Sure. I guess Lee's not available," Kenji said as he followed his friend into the security offices, where everyone was tense.

The head security guard stood over another man leaning in to try to see the screen better. This was a big screwup on their home turf, and he could tell just by glancing at all the men and women in the room that they were ticked off it had happened.

"I floated the theory that the delivery driver had to know where the cameras were," Xander said. "Hammond over there agrees, but most of them are hidden, so unless someone told him where they are…"

"Someone more than likely did. Let's see the hand-off," Kenji said, knowing that Alan Field was the top suspect as an insider working for whoever was after Daphne. Or, let's face it, the museum. That was his connection.

Part of that bothered Kenji, because the museum had been the scene of another incident. So it added something to investigate as far as Kenji was concerned. There was no way to rule out someone in Lauder's office as the suspect any more than they could rule out Field.

He leaned in closer to watch the high-quality black-and-white footage and noticed that Alan hardly glanced at the driver. Instead he was talking to a woman who stood just past the driver. The woman's face wasn't visible, but she had on a skirt and some chunky boots.

"Who's that?" Kenji asked, reaching over the video operator's shoulder and hitting Pause.

"Who?" Hammond, the security director, leaned in. "Oh, he's talking to someone else."

"Yes, any ideas who?" Xander asked him. "Those boots seem pretty distinctive."

"They do. Most of the staff here doesn't wear boots," Hammond said. "Run the tape back and see if we can identify her before the driver comes in."

Kenji stepped away from the security team while they were running the tape and tapped his earpiece.

"Van, anyone up there wearing chunky boots?"

"Give me a minute," Van said.

Kenji watched the tape from his position, hoping for a glimpse of someone he recognized from his days of watching over Daphne. He'd come into contact with a lot of people. When she walked into the frame, he caught the swing of her hair and realized she was Carl Mitchell's assistant.

Kenji was searching through his mind for her name. "Carl's assistant."

"Yes. That is Leanna," Hammond said.

"Why is she in the lobby?"

They rolled the tape forward, waiting, and saw her talk to the delivery guy and hand him something before he walked out of the building.

"We need to talk to her," Kenji said.

"I can take you to her office," Hammond said.

"I'll stay here and keep trying to identify the driver. It looks like he might have a tattoo under his left ear," Xander was saying as Kenji followed Hammond out the door.

"How long has Leanna worked for the company?" he asked the security guard.

"I couldn't tell you. I'm not entirely sure she wasn't checking on her own order," Hammond said.

"Do a lot of you order from Burger Boy?" Kenji asked.

"Yes. On Thursdays they offer the building a discount, so pretty much everyone places an order with them," Hammond said.

"Did your team?"

"Sure did. In fact, finance had a large order that came in right after the one for the fourth-floor team," Hammond said.

Kenji realized that Daphne's team was identified simply by the floor by security. "How would someone have known what cup was for Daphne?"

"They label them with our names," Hammond said. "Burgers and drinks. Fries are generic since they only serve crinkle cut."

"But everything else can be personalized?"

"Yeah. Dude, haven't you ever had Burger Boy?"

"No," he said. He wasn't much on fatty foods, plus he was usually working or enjoying his downtime in his apartment, where he ate salads and burritos.

Hammond shrugged as they got on the elevator to go to Mitchell's office. "Do the elevators have cameras?"

"They do," Hammond said.

Kenji unmuted his earpiece. "Xander, check the elevators to see if Field messed with the food on his way up."

"Will do. The delivery guy has a tattoo of a hawk below his left ear, Lee. Can you run a check for priors?"

"With that detailed description?" Lee fired back.

"Well, that's all I have. The guy is good at not being seen," Xander said.

Kenji muted the discussion and turned back to Hammond. "Do you usually have the same delivery person?"

"We have some regulars, but there is always someone new. On Thursdays, with so many orders, we just look for the Burger Boy hat and tee, and of course if they have food. No one is allowed up into the offices or even out of the main lobby," Hammond said. "I can't believe this slipped by us."

"This was well-planned. I should have thought ahead and not allowed outside food," Kenji said. Was it just the distraction of being around Daphne, or had he gotten lax? The fact was, he knew that whoever was after her was stepping up the intensity of their attacks. He should have anticipated this.

"Thanks for that. Still don't like it when someone gets injured on my watch," Hammond said.

"Me either."

Hammond led the way into Mitchell's office, and it was clear from the moment they spoke to Leanna that she was rattled and unsettled. Which didn't mean she'd helped whoever had attempted to poison Daphne. But it didn't clear her either.

From what Kenji observed, everyone in Mitchell and Partners was rattled. And given that a lot of the cases the firm represented were high-profile and sometimes controversial, he understood why everyone would be tense.

Which made it harder to figure out who was working with someone on the outside to silence Daphne.

Chapter 19

Daphne looked at the door each time it opened, waiting for Kenji. Finally, after she gave her statement to Detective Miller, he was there. She took half a step toward him before realizing what she was doing.

He was her bodyguard, not her boyfriend. She had to lace her hands together to keep from reaching for him. Kenji came over to her and put his hand on her shoulder. Their eyes met, and she knew—knew—that he wanted to touch her too.

"Are you okay?"

"Yes. Cass is the one who drank the poison," Daphne said. "I want to go and see her. Can you take me to the hospital?"

He nodded. "Let me speak to Van. Get your stuff together."

She made sure to stay in his line of sight as she walked to the end of the conference room table past Alan, who was slumped into himself. It was disheartening to see him this way. And she wanted to believe it was simply coincidence that he'd been the one to place and collect the order.

But Cass was in the hospital, and this was no game that whoever was after her was playing. It was time to stop worrying about everyone else and put her security at the top of the list.

"I thought you trusted me," Alan said.

She turned to face him and realized he'd been watching her the entire time. "This is more than trust. Cass was poisoned."

"I know that. Do you honestly think I would do it?" he asked her.

"Someone did. That's all I know. Since it was my cup, I know I didn't do it, and everyone else was in here. You have a right to be upset about being questioned, but anyone who'd collected the order would be in your shoes. It's not about you."

Justice and the law weren't perfect, but she had always tried to be impartial, and she knew that the cops were too. The only reason Alan was acting like this was…well, she wasn't one hundred percent, but she figured he was upset because she knew he had a connection to Lauder and the museum. When last she'd spoken to him, she'd been satisfied with his answers, but today had changed things.

Had she been kidding herself that Alan was like her and wanted to ensure that antiquities that had been seized or stolen were returned to their proper owners?

"I get that. I do. But it feels personal."

"I think everyone is scared right now. We order from Burger Boy all the time," Daphne said.

"Yeah."

"I think we shouldn't order in anymore," Pam said, coming over to sit down next to Alan. "I mean, I don't want to."

"Yeah, I think I'll be bringing my own food until this case goes before the judge," Daphne said.

She moved on, leaving the two of them chatting. Kenji came over to her. "Want any help?"

"No. I like to put files in my bag a certain way. I'll need to pack up Cass's stuff too," Daphne said.

"Take your time," he said when he noticed her trembling hands.

"I can't. I want to get to Cass and see that she's okay for myself. And…" She scanned the room to make sure no one was looking at them or could hear her. "I want to be alone with you. I need a hug."

"I need to hug you," Kenji said. "Let me help. You can sort your files later."

She nodded. His hand brushed hers, and a shiver of awareness went through her. She needed more than comfort at this moment. She needed more than safety. What she needed was Kenji. Holding her, making love to her, reassuring her that she was alive and that he was going to keep her that way.

Working quickly, they packed up both bags, and Daphne slung Cass's purse over her shoulder with her own. Kenji carried both of the work bags as Daphne turned to the room. Her staff were still in standby mode, some of them giving statements to the cops.

"I wish I could give everyone the afternoon off, but we need to keep working. You can do it from home if you'd rather. Send me whatever you find by the end of the day. I'm going to see Cass. I'll let you know if she wants visitors."

Everyone on her team hugged her on the way out, even Alan, but that just made her more uneasy. Someone had alerted the person who was trying to stop her about the order. That meant if it wasn't Alan, then someone else on her team was leaking information about her.

But who?

As hard as it had been to suspect Alan, he was the newest member of her team. The others had worked with her for years, and Daphne considered them friends. She wanted to believe there was nothing that would allow them to betray her.

Since Cass had been poisoned, she knew that someone had.

As soon as they were in the elevator by themselves, Kenji brushed his hand against the back of hers. She started to turn toward him. He gripped her hand hard.

"There are cameras."

He said it without moving his lips. She'd forgotten about them. She turned her hand and squeezed his before rubbing it on her skirt.

As soon as they were outside, she wanted to throw herself into his arms, but they were still in public. It wasn't that she cared about what other people thought of their relationship, but she didn't want to give them anything else to talk about.

Once they were at his car, the black Dodge Charger that she'd spent too much time in, he finally leaned over and pulled her into his arms. She hugged him tightly, putting her head on his shoulder and letting her guard down.

"I was talking to Cass when she collapsed. Why would someone do that to her?"

"They wanted to do it to you."

It seemed impossible that he'd forgotten how striking Daphne was in person, but on the drive back to her office, somehow he had. The thought of losing her had him seeing her again for the first time.

She had thick black eyebrows that framed her intelligent brown eyes. She had long, straight hair that hung halfway down her back. Though she had a reputation for being tough as nails, she always looked so ladylike and feminine. Today she had her hair pulled back, revealing the delicate shells of her ears and pearl earrings he knew her father had given her when she graduated from high school.

She never really spoke of her mom, which Kenji hadn't questioned. Their relationship had been full of passion and burned fast. There hadn't been time to dig deep into either of their pasts, something he knew appealed to him.

Today she wore a gorgeous light yellow sheath dress that went well with her coloring. It had leather at the collar and as a cuff on the short sleeves. Then a leather accent that ran across her chest. She had on hose because they was something she always wore and a pair of black leather heels that looked impossibly high and difficult to walk in but made her long legs seem even longer.

Her mouth was full, and she wore a shade of reddish-brown lipstick that he knew was close to her natural lip color. She watched him as if she wasn't sure how to react, and he didn't blame her. She had to be shocked to see him.

Actually, on second glance, he saw the signs of fatigue and pain on her face. Something fierce and primitive stirred in him. He wanted to find the person who shot at them and mete out the kind of justice he knew that Daphne would frown on.

She licked her lips, and his eyes tracked the motion. Another primitive emotion stirred in him. He still found her attractive, which wasn't a shock at all. The intensity of that desire was.

Knowing how close someone had come to poisoning her made him scared.

"We have so much to discuss," she said, shifting back to her seat. "Did you see the Director?"

That she was worried about that meeting made him realize he wasn't the only one catching feels. It was reassuring but at the same time heightened his awareness that he had to do everything in his power to protect her. He put the car in gear and started driving toward the hospital.

"I did. She wanted me to work a contact that turned out to be Nick. It involves an illegal art ring who contacted him, maybe because of the piece he purchased legally that's from the Maqdala collection? Anyway, I went to see Nick and instead suggested the agency send an operative in his place."

"What if it is connected to my case? Will the Director be able to tell us what's up for auction?" Daphne asked.

"I'm not sure. But I can ask her. I don't want to get sucked into that world."

"That's easier said than done," Daphne said. "When I was at The Hague, I was approached."

"You were?" he asked, not really surprised. She'd been a candidate they'd recruited and wanted, so even though she'd walked away, the CIA would have kept their eye on her.

"Yeah, I said no. But it was hard," she said.

"I said no. It wasn't hard for me. I won't let her manipulate me into doing anything," he said.

"You know it doesn't work like that," she said. "What if you go and I went with you."

"Are you kidding me? Someone is actively trying to kill you. Plus you're not exactly unknown to that world. I don't want you in any more jeopardy."

"I won't be with you by my side. Just think about it."

He clenched his jaw and kept his eyes forward. "I have. The answer is no."

He wasn't going to think about it more. Not for a single second. He didn't want anyone he cared for in danger. He certainly wasn't going to bring Daphne along on a mission.

They pulled into the hospital parking lot where Daphne's friend had been taken. She had been texting with her friend. When he put the car in Park and turned to her, she stopped him before they could get out.

"Cass's husband, Gerry, is up there with her. I'm here as her friend, so no pictures or the third degree. Got it?"

"Fine. But I'm going to memorize their features so I can have Lee run them.".

"I mean it, Kenji. It's bad enough that she drank the poison meant for me. These people are my closest friends, and I don't want to do anything else to make this day harder."

"I'll be on my best behavior."

"That's all I ask," she said.

Kenji got out of the car first, happy that Daphne waited for him to come and get her door. When she stepped out, he took a moment to look around the parking lot. There were too many people going in and out for him to feel safe, so he hurried her inside and up to the room where her friend waited.

Daphne's worry was clear on her face when they walked into the room. The husband rushed over to hug Daphne and then offered his hand to Kenji. "She's sleeping but doing much better."

"I'm so sorry, Gerry."

"It's not your fault. Cass has said that every time she wakes up. 'Make sure D knows it wasn't her fault.'"

"Of course she'd say that. But I'm the one whose life has been threatened. I should have thought ahead and not ordered food or shared it with her."

Kenji realized how hard Daphne was taking this. "You couldn't have known. Van is the best in the business, and even he didn't raise a flag when you ordered."

He could tell that Daphne still hadn't forgiven herself. They stayed until Cass woke up, and the two women talked and cried and hugged each other. Seeing them together made Kenji realize that it was time they stopped playing defense. It was time to go on the offense.

When they got back to Price Tower, both of them changed, and Kenji was waiting for her when she came out of the bedroom. "I have an idea, and I'm not sure if you're going to like it."

"I wish I had one. Carl asked to have the court date moved up, and I should hear something tomorrow. Which reminds me. when I was talking to Laverne at the museum, I noticed a note that said *C. 4 pm.* Did we check Carl?"

"Your boss?" Kenji asked. "I believe so. Let me ping Lee about it."

Kenji sent Lee a message and then put his phone on the table, leaning toward her. "I found Grey Joy today."

"Great. I want to talk to her. She's the person who called me and set up the meeting where I got shot," Daphne said. "I've gone over her voice and everything that happened at the archives in my head, and I'm sure of it."

"She's definitely not telling us something, and questioning her should be our next move," Kenji said. "I'd like to do it in a public place and set up a sting. See if she's working with the shooter. It would mean putting you in what seems like a very open situation."

"I'm the bait? Well, I guess I have been since the beginning. Did you ever find anything from the camera behind the coffee shop?"

"No, it had been turned off. Lee said that she noticed a pattern for turning the cameras off and alerted the cops. Apparently that alleyway is used for drug deals. So she suspects Grey might have known that or hadn't considered that there would be cameras."

Daphne pulled her notebook closer to her and then jotted down what Kenji was telling her. That really didn't tell her anything else about Grey except she might have bought drugs back there or felt safe because of the staffer she knew.

"Detective Miller has been down to talk to the other shop owners. No one saw or heard anything the night you were shot. We still don't know who the shooter was. But we do know that the caliber of bullet that fired at you was a 9mm which are used in Glocks."

"The same model as the one used to shoot at the car," Daphne said.

"Yes. No one on your staff has weapons training except for Carl and Pam."

"Pam?" she asked. It was hard to imagine Carl or Pam as the one who shot at her in the alleyway. Like it was almost impossible. She couldn't picture either of them holding a weapon.

"Yes. She has a conceal permit and goes to the range on the weekends with her husband."

How did she not know that? She'd had so many conversations with Pam, and none of them had involved that. But to be fair, they only talked about work. Pam kept her personal life very private. "Interesting."

"Yes. Also, she was the most emotional and nervous when I took her photo, and today when Cass was shot. Do you think she's involved? She is your secretary."

"She's my legal secretary. She does a lot more than keep my calendar."

"Does she have access to it?" Kenji asked.

"Yes. Actually, anyone who works at Mitchell and Partners can view my calendar. Though I didn't put the meeting with Grey on there. But I did message my team that I had a lead. So perhaps that was an alert?"

"Probably. A lot of people know where you are all the time. Is your address in the company directory?" Kenji asked.

"Yes. But anyone could type my name into a search engine and find it," Daphne said. Pam had no reason to want to harm her.

"Very true. I'm not accusing her of anything, but it seems to me that someone had to know your team was ordering out today," Kenji said.

"Everyone—"

"I already heard it from Carl's assistant. Many teams order in on Thursdays because of the discount. But someone knew when you ordered and which driver to knock out."

Daphne didn't like the facts that Kenji was presenting, but she couldn't argue with them. He was careful to be logical, and she suspected he was trying to keep her from defending her colleagues. It was working.

Someone had to have passed on the information for their order. "So we have Alan and Janice at my place, maybe Carl. But I think that's a long shot."

"Agreed," Kenji said.

She put her pen down and leaned toward him, taking his hands in hers. "What is it you are suggesting?"

He turned his hands under hers and rubbed his thumb over her knuckles. "That you let everyone on your team know you are meeting with Grey Joy. Then see what happens."

"What if Grey is a whistleblower?" Daphne asked. "Should we warn her?"

But she knew the answer to that before she asked it. They couldn't alert anyone to their plan. Right now the only people she was certain weren't trying to kill her were Kenji, Cass and Gerry.

That was it. Which left too many people at her office and at the museum that she'd spoken to about this case.

"Okay. How would it work?" she asked.

"I'd have to get my entire team involved, but I wanted to discuss this with you first. It will be dangerous," he warned her.

"That's fine. If we are successful, maybe we can revisit going to Madness for your old boss."

"Never. If we are successful, I plan to discuss us dating again."

"You do?"

"Yes."

She licked her lips and smiled over at him. "I'd like that."

"Me too," he said.

Chapter 20

That she was open to dating him again was all he wanted. There was a lot of work to do, but while they were safe at the tower, he wanted this chance to take her into his arms and make love to her. Not because she was reacting to fear and danger but because she wanted him.

He still held her hand in his and turned it over, drawing a shape on her palm. Her fingers curled around his hand.

"Kenji...will you make love to me?"

"Yes," he said, his voice low and guttural. He stood and walked to her side of the table, then put his hands on her waist and lifted her up. She had changed into a skirt with a slit on the side, and he couldn't resist running his hand up it. Her soft skin under his fingers smelled of peaches and another musk that was all Daphne. *Seductive* and *sensual* were the two words he always associated with her. Just being in her presence made him hot and hard.

His fingers shook as he touched her, slowly moving his hand up the inside of her thigh, her legs parting as his caresses traveled up until he felt the heat from her sex. With his hand on her waist, the both of them still fully dressed, he looked down into her wide brown eyes. Her lips were parted and her eyes half-lidded.

How did I ever leave her when I was younger?

He bent until he could kiss her, driving his tongue into her mouth when she wrapped her arms around him. He was so damned horny for her. Seeing her safe in his apartment had made him slip on the leash he normally used to control his base instincts. But it was gone. As her tongue slid along his, he could only suck it deeper as the gnawing ache inside of him grew. He finally had her spread out on the table in front of him.

He tore his mouth from hers, his breath sawing in and out. He groaned and stopped thinking about anything but his thickening erection and how much he wanted her.

She wore a silky blouse that clung to her chest, revealing her erect nipples. She arched her back as he drew the hand on her waist up her body, her breasts thrusting toward him. He palmed her other breast as he leaned down and sucked one nipple into his mouth through her blouse.

She moaned his name. He felt her hands in his hair, tracing the shape of his ear before moving down his neck again, caressing his chest and undoing the buttons of his shirt, then pulling the tie from his neck. Her fingers were cool against the warmth of his skin. He lifted his head from her breast and stepped back, undoing his pants and pushing them down his legs.

She stood, pulled her blouse up over her head and tossed it on the floor. Her bra followed, and Kenji caught his breath as she bent forward to take off the knee-high boots she wore and her breasts swayed forward.

He reached out to fondle her as she undid the waistband of her skirt. With a shimmy, pushed it down her hips and onto the floor.

She shoved her panties down and stepped out of them, totally, gloriously naked in front of him.

Their eyes met, and she smiled. "Remember the first time?"

He groaned. "I wanted you so much I could hardly wait until you were naked."

"That's right. You were in before I finished taking my panties off."

He got even harder when she mentioned that fact. She held her hand out, and he stepped forward. His cock jutted in front of him, and she took him in her hand, grasping his shaft and pulling him closer to her.

There was no hiding his reaction to her. And he didn't want to. For the first time since she'd come back in his life, he felt like he'd found his purpose. Protecting her and everyone in the family he'd created for himself.

Every breath he took was filled with the scent of her. The feel of her under his fingers inflamed every sense in his body. He was compelled by the need to fill her completely. Putting his hands on her waist, he lifted her up and turned until he could set her down on the table. He stepped between her legs, tangling his hands in her long silky hair, tugging lightly on it until her head fell back, exposing the long length of her neck. He kissed it.

Tasting that creamy expanse, he moved his mouth slowly down the elegant length of it. He brushed a strand of her hair aside with his nose, continuing to kiss her skin.

She wrapped her arms around his shoulders and

tightened her legs around his hips. Her response to him was addicting, and he craved more of her reactions.

He put his hands on her legs, caressing her knees and slowly moving his hands down her left leg until he got to her foot. He lifted her foot and placed it in the center of his chest. She wriggled her toes against him, and he caressed the arch of her foot.

He ran his finger along her instep, tickling her, and she squirmed. All thoughts of small feet and tickling dropped away. He glided his fingers up her leg. It was strong, muscled from years of walking in high heels, he suspected.

There was so much strength in all of her. The last few days would have broken the strongest of men, but she just kept powering on. Not looking for a shortcut or an easy way out but putting herself right in the middle of the action. She was willing to do it again, making herself the bait.

It was only his confidence in himself to keep her safe and in her to keep her nerve that had even made him suggest it.

He lowered his mouth, kissing and nibbling his way up her other leg until once again his head was buried between her legs. He mouthed her. Her thighs tightened around his head, and then she let them fall open.

Her hair was neatly trimmed, and he parted her with his fingers. Her flesh was a delicate pink and the little nub at the center swollen with need. He gently caressed her. Her hips shifted a little bit left to right. He touched her in a circular motion, and she moaned. A sound of approval. He continued to move his finger over her before he leaned down closer.

He exhaled hard watching her legs fall wider apart as she lifted her hips toward Kenji, presenting her body to him. She grabbed his head, and her legs undulated next to him, one of them falling over his shoulder as he licked at her delicate flesh. He traced her core with his finger, just teasing the opening, and then slowly pushed one finger up inside of her. Her hips jerked upright, and he continued to eat her. She was delicious.

He added a second finger inside of her and thrust them deep and deeper. This was what he needed. To taste her and feel her passion before they both left this apartment and he put her out there for someone to try to hurt.

He was rock-hard, his cock straining to be inside of her, but he wanted to make this moment last as long as he could. He continued moving his mouth over her until he felt her body start to tighten around his fingers, kept rocking them in and out of her until she arched her back and cried his name.

He lifted his head, pulled his fingers from her body and looked up at her. She was on her elbows, gazing down at him. Her eyes were fiery, passionate. There was a flush to her body, and her breath flowed in and out, causing her breasts to rise and fall rapidly.

He felt her hand rubbing up and down his cock. He jerked forward and realized his control was more slippery than he'd imagined. She traced his length, her fingernail scraping over his skin. He loved the feel of her hand on his naked shaft.

She took his shaft in one hand, stroking him in her fist. Moving it up and down in a slow and sensuous movement that made his balls tighten. She skimmed her finger over the tip of his erection, and his hips jerked forward.

She cupped his sac in one hand and squeezed very softly as she tightened her grip on his shaft. He started to thrust in her hand. She leaned in, and he felt her breath on his erection a moment before her tongue dashed out and traced the tip of him.

Sensation shivered up and down his spine, and he canted his hips forward, feeling her mouth engulf him. He tried to control himself. He'd been lauded for his self-control, but her mouth made a mockery of that. He was thrusting into her mouth, his hands in her hair and her hands on his balls.

He didn't want to come until he was inside of her and pulled her up his body, pushing her back until she was supine on the table. Then he leaned forward over her. He shoved his hand into her hair and brought his mouth down on hers as he shifted his hips and entered in one long thrust. Heat burned between them as they drove themselves harder and harder, until he felt her body tightening around his cock. He held her hips hard against him as he continued to thrust up into her until he felt his balls tighten. And he came, and her along with him. He emptied himself as he continued to thrust into her until he was spent.

He held her in his arms on the table in his living room, resting his head against her breasts and knowing that he would do anything he had to in order to keep Daphne in his life. He needed her more than he'd wanted to admit out loud, but his soul already knew the importance of this woman.

He felt her hand stroking his neck and shoulders and

lifted himself so he could see her face. She gave him that soft, gentle smile, and he knew that whether he wanted to say the words or not, he had more than feelings for Daphne. He loved her.

He had loved this woman probably from the first time he'd seen her back in college. He'd loved her when he left her. He'd loved her when he'd been in the world doing unspeakable things. And he still loved her now.

The only thing he wasn't sure of was if he was worthy of her love. He knew he'd do whatever he had to in order to keep her safe. Not the right or moral thing, the thing that would keep her alive no matter what.

That wasn't a choice Daphne would approve of, but there it was.

"I wanted you from the moment you walked into my conference room," she said.

"Did you?"

"Yes. I was so happy to see you, and I felt like I could finally breathe. I thought, *Kenji's here. I'm safe.*"

He buried his face in her shoulder and hugged her tightly to him. "I will always keep you safe."

That vow was one he'd never allow himself to break. And if he felt himself slipping toward that monster he'd been when he'd worked for the agency, he'd do the right thing and walk away from her. Because Daphne safe and healthy was the only thing that could make him feel okay.

"Kenji?"

I love you, Daphne. He thought it, but didn't allow himself to say it out loud.

Chapter 21

Daphne was still trying to process everything that had happened between her and Kenji when they were called to Lee's office and the conference room area. She wore a pair of ripped jeans and a Christmas sweater that she and Cass had bought together for their Black Friday not-shopping day. She and Cass always went on a hike the day after Thanksgiving, and Gerry came with them if he was able to. Because Gerry was an ER doctor, his schedule wasn't always set. This year it had been just her and Cass.

She sensed that Kenji was having second thoughts about using her as bait. Mainly because he held her hand when they were in the elevator, and that wasn't something he normally would have done.

"We should talk about us," she said.

"After the meeting. Detective Miller got a set of prints from the censer that weren't yours. Van asked Nick if they could see whether there were any prints on the shield he bought at auction, and he agreed."

"Thank you for doing that," she said. "I never thought to ask the cops to dust anything for prints."

"After the poisoning at your office today, Detective Miller mentioned they are ramping up their efforts to try to catch whoever is after you," Kenji said. "Not that they weren't before, but the cops are overworked. It helps that Nick is family so we could easily get the item."

"Will he be at the meeting?"

"Both he and Luna will be. Everyone on the team is going to be there. I think you've met them all except maybe Rick."

She nodded. "You're right, I haven't met Rick. Before we go in there, please know that I'm not going to be swayed from putting myself up as bait."

Kenji put his hand on the back of her neck and brought his mouth down on hers hard and fast. She kissed him back just as fiercely. He might not like her putting herself in danger, but she hated the thought of him doing it as well.

He lifted his head just as the elevator doors opened. "I know."

"Good," she said, squeezing his hand as they walked into the room and found the group waiting along with Detective Miller.

She caught them up on the prints she'd found, which she had a team running through the database. She'd also given Lee a copy, which she was running through the international databases she had access to through her connections. So Lee was at her computer.

"I have a quicker way to find Daphne's attacker," Kenji said as they all sat down.

"We have an idea," Daphne said, not willing to be sidelined. Now that Cass had been poisoned in her place and she realized that winning the case was going to take too long to stop the threat to both herself and those she cared about, she was determined to do whatever she could to stop it herself.

"Let's hear it," Van said, leaning forward and lacing his fingers together.

Daphne cleared her throat. "I think the informant who called me was Grey Joy. Her voice was very familiar, and when I started to question her at the museum, I think she was about to confirm she was the contact before we were attacked."

"I've located Grey Joy with Lee's help, and we'd like to set up a meeting in a public place," Kenji said. "The rest of us would be in position to keep the women safe but also to observe who else is in the area. Daphne doesn't believe anyone on her staff could be complicit in the attacks on her."

"I don't. But Kenji pointed out that one of my paralegals has a permit to carry a concealed weapon, and so does my boss. He's suggested I add the meeting to my calendar so everyone with access will know about it."

"That's a lot to take in. Are you ruling out the museum?" Detective Miller said.

Daphne wasn't. "Detective Miller, I wondered if you could let them know that I found the censer the night I was shot and that I am meeting with my contact to try to find more missing items."

Detective Miller made some notes on the narrow pad in front of her. "I can do that. When is this meeting?"

"I haven't set it up yet," Daphne admitted.

"The police should be there as well," Detective Miller said. "If I can make it, I will. If not, I can ask for someone from the art team."

"That would be great," Daphne said. "I'm hoping to record Grey's statement to use in court. But I need her to trust me. I'm not entirely sure why she didn't stay in the alleyway that night."

"Perhaps she only planned for you to find the item," Rick said from the corner of the table. "When I worked for the DEA, that was a common practice so that you couldn't really identify each other."

Honestly, she'd thought the man was on the verge of falling asleep. Van nodded at Rick.

"I hadn't considered that. But it makes sense," Daphne said. "I guess I need to call Grey first and get her to agree to meet me."

Kenji leaned in. "We need to know where you are going to meet. It needs to be a place busy enough that we all won't stick out but are protected."

"Do you have an idea in mind?" Van asked Kenji.

"Zara's Brew—the coffee shop with the alleyway where Daphne was first meant to meet her. It's in North Hollywood and has a large glass window front but walls on three sides. There is only one small hallway with a unisex bathroom and an exit door. Easy to keep them safe inside."

"Plus lots of vantage points. Bulletproof glass?" Van asked.

"Doubtful," Detective Miller said.

The team started talking about logistics that Daphne didn't need to be a part of. She'd committed to this, and there was no turning back. She could only hope that no one on her team was part of it. She hated to think that she'd been naive or that she'd put others in danger.

Even though this had been his idea, Kenji didn't like it. Daphne had spoken on the phone with Grey, who'd agreed to meet at Zara's Brew in North Hollywood the next morning at ten. He noticed Nick and Daphne talking and knew she wanted to find out more about the provenance that had come with the shield when he purchased it and the illegal auction he'd been invited to attend. But it was just listed as an item from the Hazelton-Measham collection, and the grandson, Thomas, was listed as the one selling it.

"Did anyone on your team speak to Thomas?" Kenji asked.

"I think Pam was meant to call him," Daphne said. "Let me ping her. Should I mention in the chat that I'm speaking to Grey tomorrow?"

"Might as well," Kenji said.

Daphne started typing out the message on her phone, and Nick turned to Kenji. "Regarding the other matter we discussed, I have the time and place for the auction."

"I'll pass the information along," Kenji said.

"Have you reconsidered you and me going?" she asked him.

"No," he said firmly.

Daphne pulled him away from Nick and the others to a corner of the room. "If we are going to be together, then we have to be a part of each other's lives. You've gotten a good glimpse at my job. I want a chance to know your world too."

"I want you safe."

She put her hand on his cheek. "This isn't going to be the last threat to either of us. I'll take another high-profile case. You'll guard someone who is at risk. Our lives aren't going to be safe."

Kenji didn't like her assessment, but he knew that she had a point. "What if you don't like it or get tired—"

"I'm not going to do that. I didn't want to join the agency because I knew we'd be separated and working different missions. Maybe never seeing each other. The fact that we will be able to come home to each other— that is all I need."

"Are you sure?"

"I think so. I mean, I didn't like it when I thought you were shot , but with your team around us…" She trailed off. Kenji realized that she really didn't have any idea of how dangerous this mission she'd agreed to was.

There was a chance that they caught the bad guy and she got hurt. He vowed to himself again that he wouldn't let anything happen to her. He knew he could keep her safe. That was the only thing he wanted to do.

"Sorry to interrupt, but you're needed, Kenji," Xander said, coming over to them.

Kenji nodded and straightened his tie before he walked back over to his boss. Van clapped a hand on his shoulder as he arrived. "You'll be on Daphne. I want someone watching the informant too, but I'm not sure two bodyguards in the coffee shop won't give the game away."

Kenji understood they all carried themselves in a manner that was different from people just getting coffee.

"I can do it," Rick said. "Unless you wanted me on the alley? I blend way better than you lot do."

"Hey, I can blend," Luna argued.

"You can, but you are better at being sociable," he reminded her. "Someone is going to have to be behind the counter with the barista."

"True," Luna agreed.

"So you two will be in the shop. Rick, get there when they open and set up near the front. Luna, the barista has agreed you can shadow her for the day. You're doing research for a book," Van said.

Luna and Rick both nodded. Xander and Lee were still awaiting assignments, and Kenji was sure Van would be close by.

"I'm going to hang with Miller's cops. Lee's on over-watch, and Xander, you take the alleyway," Van said. "Bulletproof vests on everyone including Daphne, and earpieces as well."

He glanced at Daphne and noticed her face seemed a little paler. It was one thing to imagine being bait in a sting. It was something else entirely to get ready to do it. He worried about her reaction, but she just stood up straighter and nodded at him.

His heart beat a little faster. He loved her for her courage and her strength, especially when she was afraid. It was one of the many things he admired about her. She had thrown him when she'd mentioned wanting to see what he did.

He didn't want her anywhere near his world, but he knew she wouldn't be satisfied with anything less. She wasn't going to just be a woman he came home to. He wasn't sure how he felt about that. He might have this found family at Price Security, but there had always been a part of himself he kept hidden from everyone else.

Daphne felt like it was obvious she had the bullet-proof vest on under her clothes. But she had checked herself in the full-length mirror twice and knew it wasn't visible. Today she'd dressed in a one of her A-line skirts, a shirt that she could blouse out a bit and a blazer. She had her favorite Louboutin heels and her bag that she carried everywhere with her.

Kenji was waiting for her when she came out. He was in total bodyguard mode, his face serious, his body tense. But he smiled when he saw her. "Ready?"

No, who in their right mind would be ready for this? "Yes, of course. I'm ready to hear what Grey has to say."

"Good," he said. "Will the judge allow you to submit the recorded conversation?"

"Yes. I'll tell her she's being recorded and have her acknowledge it. It will be fine."

Kenji nodded, and Daphne wondered if he was nervous. "It'll be okay. I trust you to keep us safe."

Kenji gave her a tight smile, and she realized nothing she said to him was going to put him at ease. Her phone pinged as they headed down to the car. Janice was running late to work, and Pam was going to stop by the courthouse to drop off the brief she'd finished the night before.

Daphne asked to approve it first, but Pam had set her status to Not Available in their Slack chat. Kenji drove them to the coffee shop, and they arrived a few minutes early. She glanced around the parking lot but didn't see any of the other Price Security team or the cops.

Which she guessed was a good thing. They were meant to be hidden, and she knew that with Kenji by her side, she'd be fine, or as fine as she could be.

"When we get out, we'll follow the protocols. Inside you just do your job, get the information from Grey you need, and allow me to do my job."

"I will," she said, and stopped him before he could get out of the car. Leaning over, she pulled him close. "Don't forget to keep yourself safe too."

"I won't," he said.

Then he opened the door, and she took a deep breath, knowing this was the moment that she'd get the answers she'd been waiting for. This was it. They walked slowly across the parking lot. When they got inside, the booth that she and Kenji had sat in before was taken, and he frowned as he had to take one in front of the windows. She noticed Rick was slouched in the corner of one of the booths in the middle of the shop, and the booth next to him was available.

"That one. Sit on the left," he said, which put her on the same side as Rick's booth.

She slipped into it. Kenji hesitated, and she knew he was debating if he could leave her to get coffee for them. "It has to look normal. I'll have a peppermint latte."

"Watch me, and if I gesture, you get under that table."

"Of course." She didn't want to be killed, so she was going to take every order that she was given seriously.

The door opened as Kenji got in line, and Daphne noticed Grey's silver bob as she entered. The other woman glanced furtively around before spotting Daphne. She hurried over to her and slid onto the bench across from her.

"Morning," Daphne said. "Thank you for agreeing to meet me. Would you like a drink?"

"Cappuccino," she said.

Kenji, who'd come back for Grey's drink order, nodded. "Be right back. Remember what I said."

"I do."

Daphne had a form for Grey to sign acknowledging that she knew her statement was being taped and that she was telling the truth.

"I need you to sign this form as we discussed last night so I can use your testimony in my filings. You will be called into court to testify that these statements are yours and that they are the truth. Are you still willing to talk to me?" Daphne asked.

"I am," Grey said. "This has been going on for too long."

"Don't start talking yet. Let me get the voice recorder open on my phone," Daphne said. "Would you mind wearing one of my Airpods so I can get a clearer sound of your voice? The ambient noise in here is very loud."

Grey held out her hand, and Daphne put the left pod in it. She put in her right pod so that both of their voices would be recorded.

"This is Daphne Amana, counsel for Marjorie Wyman, representative of the culture office of Amba Mariam in the case regarding the ownership of the Hazelton-Measham collection.

"I am here with…state your name."

"Grey Joy."

"Who works for…"

"The Los Angeles Museum of Foreign Cultures as an archivist."

"For how long?"

"I've worked there for fifteen years."

Daphne wanted to get to the missing items, but she knew she had to build who Grey was so that Judge Mallon would allow the testimony. "What does your job entail?"

Grey sort of scrunched up her nose and shrugged. "Everything really. I catalog all of the items that are brought in and out of the archives."

Kenji was making his way back to them with a tray that had their drinks on it. She noticed he was watching the restaurant and the sidewalk outside.

"Did there come a time when you became aware of the Hazelton-Measham collection?" Daphne asked her.

"Yes—"

Grey broke off talking, slumping forward as Kenji dropped the tray and Rick sprang to life. Daphne was still processing that the other woman had been shot as Kenji reached her side and was hit with a bullet in the shoulder. He fell to the ground, dragging her to the floor with him.

Kenji hugged her close, pushing her under the table, and Rick was at his side as Kenji ordered her to stay there and took off in the direction of the shooter.

Chapter 22

Adrenaline pumping, Kenji ran full out in the direction of the shooter. He didn't let the graze to his shoulder affect him as he pushed through the panicked people in the coffee shop and ran straight across the parking lot. Xander was hot on Kenji's heels, and two undercover cops were behind.

Kenji had been trained as an operative, but he'd also taken extra combat training, and he drew on that now. He and Xander kept each other honed by working out all the time, something he barely acknowledged as he raced full-on to find the shooter.

He wasn't letting this man get away. Unlike the car, where he'd had to keep Daphne safe, this time he knew she'd be taken care of, and there was nothing that would stop him. This time the shot had been too close. In his mind, he saw Daphne lying forward with the blood coming out of her chest instead of Grey Joy.

This ends now.

Scanning the area where he thought the shot had come from, Kenji spotted a man in camo running toward the highway. Days of waiting and investigating were over, giving him an extra burst of speed.

He was gaining quickly on the other man, who was

carrying a rifle case in one hand and had a Glock in the other. The shooter turned and fired wide but still close to Kenji. Kenji used the man's distraction and didn't hesitate.

Gathering his energy, Kenji took a flying kick toward the man, hitting him square in the back and knocking him to the ground. Kenji also hit the ground on the side where he'd been shot and groaned as he rolled and got to his feet. The other man stood up too, throwing his rifle bag to the ground. He hit Kenji with a solid left hook to the arm that was bleeding where he'd been shot.

Kenji hit the man hard in the throat. Then he lifted his leg in a forward front kick and brought it down hard on the shooter's neck, knocking him backward. Kenji followed with a one-two punch to his jaw and then hit him hard in the gut, driving the other man to the ground before kicking him backward. He came down with his full weight on the other man's chest. The man put his hands up by his shoulders and stayed in position.

"I'm here," Xander said, sliding up next to Kenji.

"Search him. He dropped the rifle over there, and I think he had a Glock." A professional would have more weapons on him. Kenji wasn't sure how long he could hold the assailant, but with Xander next to him, he was sure they'd be able to keep him here or knocked out until the cops arrived.

"Who do you work for?" Kenji asked, dropping to his knee next to the man.

The man just shook his head.

"You were the shooter in the car on the freeway?"

"Yes."

"Who was driving?"

"I'm not giving that up," he said with a hard look. "Good luck keeping that woman alive."

"Are there more contracts on her?"

He shrugged, and Kenji drew back to punch him again. But Xander stopped him. "Cops."

Kenji almost didn't let that sway him. This man was baiting him, but he must feel confident that whomever had hired him would keep him safe.

"We'll take it from here," the lead officer said. "Thanks for catching him."

"No problem. Has the ambulance arrived yet?"

"Yes. The victim is being transported to the hospital," the officer said.

Hospital, not morgue.

Daphne would never have forgiven herself if Grey had been killed in a sting that they'd set up.

"She won't be talking for a while," the shooter said.

Kenji stumbled and fell hard on the man's chest, making sure he brought the full weight of his body down when his knee connected with the body. "Sorry. Ground's slippery."

Xander offered Kenji a hand and helped him up. Kenji took more than a little satisfaction out of watching the other man struggle to breathe. As Kenji got to his feet and the cops put the other man in handcuffs, Xander and he were ready in case the shooter tried to make a break for it, but he didn't. The cops collected the dropped weapons, and then they both felt like they could move.

"You okay? That wound on your shoulder is bleeding like a mother."

"Yeah, I'm fine. I knew this would shake something loose, but I don't recognize that guy. He's not from Mitchell and Partners or the museum."

"He looks like a hired gun to me. The cops will find out who's paying him. He's not going to want to go down for this. Grey looks like she might not make it."

"I guess that's been the goal, to keep her from talking," Kenji said. But something still didn't feel right. There was more to this than he'd seen so far.

"Luna's riding with Grey to the hospital, and I'm sure Daphne will want to go with her."

"Not today. Let's get back there before she does something rash," Kenji said.

"Rick's riding herd on her," Xander said with a slight smile.

Kenji couldn't smile about anything at this moment. His shoulder hurt, and his woman had been put in danger. Once again they didn't have the person responsible. When he got back to the coffee shop, Daphne dashed into his arms.

"You scared me," she said, hugging him tightly. "You're bleeding, so I know you were shot this time."

"It's just a graze. The bullet hit the wall behind me. Other than Grey, was anyone else injured?" he asked.

"One lady fainted, but otherwise no," she said.

She called an EMT over to them and didn't let go of his hand while he was examined and had a bandage put on the wound. When they were alone, she turned to him.

"I don't like that Grey was shot before she could really talk to me. Was the shooter anyone we knew?"

"No. Hired gun."

"So all of this was for nothing," she said.

"Someone doesn't want Grey talking to you," Kenji said.

"I already knew that. I shouldn't have set her up like that," Daphne said.

"She knew what she was doing."

"You say that, but I'm pretty sure she was scared too," Daphne said. "I want to get back to my office and go through the notes I have. There must be something I've missed in all of this."

"Okay. Let's go."

"You're not going to try to talk me out of it?"

"Why would I? Like you said, there isn't anything else to find here. The cops will let us know what they find out from the shooter. Maybe it will be a name that you can use," Kenji said.

Daphne was pale, and her hand shook as she looked back at the table where her work bag and phone still sat. He nodded to Rick, and the other man got Daphne's stuff, even cleaning the blood spatter from her phone before bringing it over to them.

"Here you go," Rick said. "Sorry things got hairy."

"Thanks," Daphne said, taking her bag and phone from him. "Sorry I was difficult when Kenji left."

"No problem. I hate not being in the action too," Rick said, winking at her before he turned away.

Kenji looked over at Daphne, who held her phone gingerly. He glanced at it and noticed it was still recording. He took the phone from her and stopped it.

"Did you try to follow?"

"Yes. I told you I don't like seeing you shot at," she said.

Daphne wasn't sure that she'd ever be able to forget seeing the blood spattering from Grey's chest as the other woman slumped forward. Her hands were still shaking. Kenji stood behind her, the scent of blood mingled with his aftershave. He kept her in the shadow of his body as they moved, but she was afraid for him. He'd proved that he was going to put her life ahead of his.

She was angry that she hadn't seen this possibility when they'd set up the sting. She'd believed they'd at least have a chance to find out who was behind the attacks on her and the missing museum pieces.

She turned to say something to Kenji when she saw a black Mercedes driving too fast for the parking lot. Then she realized it was coming straight toward them, not slowing.

"Kenji!"

He saw the car just as it mounted the curb and plowed into them. Kenji wrapped his arms around her as they fell, his body taking the impact of fall to the concrete. He rolled with her until they were away from the car. Her head hurt as they stopped, and she realized she was bleeding…and so was Kenji.

She reached up to touch his face as they both heard the car door open. Kenji was clearly dazed, and Daphne looked beyond him to see Ben Cross get out of the car, holding a gun pointed at her.

The opposing counsel looked angry and not like Daphne had ever seen him before. She got to her feet.

"Ben? What's going on?" she asked, more than a little confused. Why was the lawyer trying to kill her?

"I'm here to make sure you don't ruin everything," Ben said.

"How? We are going to have our day in court, and you are a capable lawyer. I'm sure—"

"I don't want a day in court," Ben said. "I've had an agreement with Dan Jones at the museum for years that worked out just fine until you brought the case. Now everyone is looking into the Maqdala items, and my market has dried up."

"What market?"

"Selling the items back to the country that they belong to," he said, lifting his weapon and pointing it at her chest.

Daphne realized he was going to fire. She had the bulletproof vest on, so she walked a little closer as she heard Kenji curse behind her.

He shoved her to the side as he flew past her, grabbing Ben's arm and forcing it up over his head. Ben's shot went into the air as Kenji tackled him to the ground. The other man was no match for Kenji and the other members of the Price Security team along with Detective Miller, who were all streaming out of the coffee shop.

Miller handcuffed Ben and read him his rights. She also dispatched officers to pick up Dan Jones. Ben admitted that he'd kept tabs on Daphne through her paralegal, Janice, whose kids were at the same school as his sons.

They all went to the police station, where Ben further confessed to working with Dan to sell the objects back to the country they came from. Then Dan would "borrow" them back so they would remain on display. The shield that Nicholas DeVere had bought was meant for a wealthy member of the elite in Amba Mariam. Which had ticked Ben off...

Grey Joy recovered enough to admit she'd been paid to call Daphne and set up the meeting. She told them she was meant to just drop the censer so that Daphne would find it and be injured. It would seem like Daphne had stolen the item and was trying to sell it. They thought the cops would find the item with her. When Grey failed, Dan was angry with her and threatened her, and Grey realized she might be framed instead of Daphne and decided to talk to Daphne.

It was a long day and well past midnight when they left the precinct. Now that the truth was revealed, Pierce was willing to talk to Daphne about settling out of court. He was horrified to learn what Dan had been doing. Daphne was going to take a few days off and would be mediating talks between the museum and Marjorie.

Kenji stood quietly behind her while she was given all the information and their statements were taken. He had somehow had time to change into a clean suit and now leaned against the wall waiting for her. He straightened when he saw her, and her heart beat faster.

How was she going to be able to live with the risks he took? She loved him. She'd known that last night but hadn't wanted to admit it to herself or him. She wondered if she'd fallen in love with him again or if the truth was she'd never really fallen out of love with him.

Maybe the reason she'd poured herself into her work was that no man could measure up to

"You're off the hook. The danger to me is over," she said.

"Great. Where to? Your place or mine?" he asked.

"I'm not sure," she said. She needed time to think and process everything. She needed a few hours to make sure that her emotions were true and not left over from the past or the danger she'd been in.

"Really? Because I am," he said, coming closer to

her and not stopping until there wasn't even an inch of space between them.

"How can you be?" she asked him. This was hard. She was trying to do the smart thing. To prove to herself that she wasn't falling for Kenji again only because he made her feel like she was enough just as she was. That there was nothing missing inside of her.

But she knew it was more than that. He saw her, and he also accepted her. Was she willing to take the risk of loving and living with him?

She just wasn't sure.

How could he be? He didn't blame her for asking. They'd been through a lot the last few days, and it had taken a toll even on him. But for him, it had simply reinforced what he already knew. He wasn't letting go of her again. He'd admitted to himself he loved her, and he knew it was time to tell her as well.

A police station late at night wasn't exactly what he'd had in mind for when he told her he loved her, but he wasn't going to wait another second. They'd been through a lot today. He'd been shot at too many times. His shoulder throbbed from the gunshot, his chest ached from the impact of the fall he'd taken when Ben had hit them with his car. And he just wanted to be back at Price Tower secure in the knowledge that nothing could come for them while he held Daphne in his arms and made love to her and then slept.

That was what he wanted. But he had no idea what her desires were. She'd mentioned dating after her case was over. And he'd thought maybe that would work. But today had shaken her. She'd seen him in action, and she had said she wanted to see what his job was like, but he knew the reality of it was that she might not have liked it.

"Is it my job?" he asked her. That was something he wasn't sure he could change. Being a protector had been ingrained in him since childhood. He'd taken a less dangerous job, but he wasn't sure there were any other options for him.

"No. I mean, I don't love it, but you're so good at what you do, Kenji. When I saw the way you moved today, I realized how important it is that you are out there keeping everyone safe," she said.

He shoved his hand through his hair and saw that he had some dirt under his fingernails. Even Daphne didn't look as sophisticated and put together as she usually did. Her skirt had been torn when they fell to the ground outside the coffee shop, and she had a faint bruise starting on her cheekbone.

He'd done a great job at saving her life, but he wasn't sure he'd done enough to keep her safe. He'd had the idea to set her up as bait and felt so confident in himself and his team that he hadn't considered they might get their man but also allow Daphne to get hurt.

"I am. I won't quit."

"I know. I wouldn't ask you to," she said. "Truth?"

"Always."

"I'm trying to stall for time to make sure that what I feel for you is legit and not just some hangover from all those years ago," she said. "Not a pretty answer, but there it is."

"How do you feel about me?"

She chewed one side of her lip, something he'd never seen her do before, as she took a deep breath. "I love you."

She loved him.

That settled it. Whatever else needed to be sorted would work itself out. "I love you too."

He pulled her into his arms and brought his mouth on hers, kissing her with all the love that he'd kept hidden over the last few hours. There wasn't anything that would keep him from making her his. They'd work out the details of how to live together, but he knew that this time, he couldn't walk away from her.

She hugged him tightly. Turning her head, she broke their kiss, and their eyes met. "I'm not sure what to do now."

"We'll work it out together. You by my side…it's all I've ever wanted," he said.

"Not all," she said.

"I might have thought I wanted excitement and a life of adventure, but these last few days with you have proved to be more excitement, danger and adventure than the others. And loving you, Daphne—I think that will be the greatest adventure of all."

* * * * *

The Price Security team will be back in 2025.

HARLEQUIN
Reader Service

Enjoyed your book?

Try the perfect subscription for Romance readers and get more great books like this delivered right to your door.

See why over 10+ million readers have tried Harlequin Reader Service.

Start with a Free Welcome Collection with free books and a gift—valued over $20.

Choose any series in print or ebook. See website for details and order today:

TryReaderService.com/subscriptions

RSBPA24R